Vexed

IRON BULLS MC #4

VEXED

(IRON BULLS MC #4)

PHOENYX SLAUGHTER

COPYRIGHT

ABOUT VEXED

(IRON BULLS MC #4)

Falling in love will only leave you vexed.

Recent high school graduate, Athena Vale, might seem bubbly and uncomplicated, but she has big plans and even bigger dreams, she's only ever shared with her best friend, Karina. Athena's strict upbringing has left her curious about taking a walk on the wild side—just once. And she knows exactly who she wants to go wild with.

President of the Iron Bulls MC, Reed "Romeo" Crownover has no shortage of women willing to entertain him. But these days, there's only one girl on his mind—Athena. When she shows up at his clubhouse on the night of her eighteenth birthday, he decides it's time to work her out of his system.

But one night turns into two, two turns into three, and soon the no-strings fun turns into something more passionate than either of them expected. An intense romance neither of them have ever experienced or knew they wanted.

She's half his age.

He doesn't fit in her world.

She's leaving for Los Angeles to start a new life in a few days.

Their connection was vexed from the start.

VEXED

Adjective: vexed

Verb: vex

1. (of a problem or issue) difficult and much debated; problematic.

synonyms: disputed, in dispute, contested, in contention, contentious, debated, at issue, controversial.

1. annoyed, frustrated, or worried.

synonyms: annoyed, irritated, exasperated, irked, piqued, nettled, displeased, put out, disgruntled; informal aggravated, peeved, miffed, riled, hacked off, hot under the collar, teed off, ticked off, sore, bent out of shape.

ONE

ROMEO

How CAN I still be fucked up over one little girl?

Athena.

That sweet little bitch has had me acting stupid since the day her sassy ass showed up at my clubhouse.

It's Dante's fault. My Sergeant-at-Arms found himself a girl, Karina. Hot, smart, and down for about anything. Stare at her for longer than two seconds and you're asking for an up close and painful introduction to Dante's fists. My stone-faced-killer friend doesn't fuck around when it comes to his girl. It's *her* best friend I haven't been able to stop thinking about.

Tagging along with Dante to the girls' graduation yesterday didn't help. That's *high school* graduation, mind you. All I thought about was how today she'd be turning eighteen. Not even running into her uptight, upscale, bitch-faced parents had settled my dick down.

Like fuck do I plan to chase after her. Not my style. Besides, there's enough willing girls trolling my clubhouse who've been legal longer than five seconds. Any one of them will be thrilled to service me, then go away. The way I prefer my relationships. Quick and uncomplicated.

Unfortunately, my dick isn't interested in any of them. No matter how hard the girls have tried to get my attention tonight.

Spotting Dante and Karina walk in the front of door, I glance behind them. No Athena.

I'm capable of casually asking about her without sounding like a complete creep, right?

Then she stumbles in the door. With her scared little Goldilocks expression, she looks like she's about to meet up with the biggest, baddest wolf.

Me.

Dante's wearing his *I need to choke someone face.* Hooking my thumbs in my pockets, I approach the trio slowly.

"What's up?" I ask Dante, who rolls his eyes at me. He's not fooled one bit by my laid back act.

"Hi, Romeo," Karina says shyly. I still can't get over how a scary motherfucker like Dante managed to snag such a beautiful and soft-spoken chick. "Um, Athena and I spent the day with her family for her *birthday*, and she asked if she could join us tonight. I hope that's okay." I appreciate the emphasis Karina puts on the word birthday. What a nice, subtle hint that her friend's now fair game.

Finally.

"Is it your birthday, sweetheart?" I ask Athena. When I put all my attention on her, she blushes and glances at the floor. A much different reaction than I expected, considering how tough she usually acts.

"Yes."

Dante sighs and steps away from the girls. Karina leads her friend to the bar and I ain't happy about not being able to say more than a few words to the girl who's taken over my every wank fantasy for weeks now.

Taking me by the arm, Dante pulls me a few steps away. "Listen, I ain't got no say over what you do with your dick, brother. But I feel responsible for her, being she's Karina's friend and all. Treat her with care, please."

It's a lot for my Sergeant-at-Arms to say. There aren't many females he gives two fucks about. And I sure as fuck don't remember the last time I heard *please* come out of his mouth. For once, I set my sarcasm aside. "Yeah. She'll be okay with me. I won't let her out of my sight."

Dante searches my face and must finally decide I'm sincere, because he nods. We join the girls at the bar. Dante immediately pulls his girl to his side.

"Athena, we'll be upstairs. You need anything, call your girl." He tilts his head toward Karina, then drags her upstairs. Not that she protests.

Athena watches them leave, but I can't take my eyes off her. She pushes her shoulders back and slowly swivels her bar stool toward me. "Am I finally allowed to have a tour of your clubhouse, Mr. President?" she asks in a low, husky voice I don't expect from someone her age.

Seems Miss Goldilocks isn't so scared anymore.

"Come here, you," I say as I pull her closer. I spin her seat, so her back's to the bar and she has to tip her head back to see my face. Staring down into her bold, steel-blue eyes unbalances me. "Did you have a good birthday?"

"Not really. I think you can make it better, though."

I can make it better, or I can make it the biggest mistake of her young life. I shouldn't mess around with this girl. She deserves a nice guy, who isn't almost twice her age.

Except, I've wanted her from the second we met. And now there's no reason I can't have her.

Athena

All day I begged Karina to let me tag along to her boyfriend's motorcycle club, but now that I'm here, I'm terrified.

The reality is so much scarier than all the things I've fantasized about since the first time I visited the Iron Bulls MC's clubhouse.

A few weeks ago, I'd dropped Karina off to visit her boyfriend. I hadn't expected the president of the club to take an interest me. The intensity of his deep blue eyes tied my tongue in knots and I made a fool of myself. That had been during the middle of the day. Things were relatively calm.

Tonight, the clubhouse is in the middle of a big celebration, and I've never seen some of the sex acts being done around me. Not even on those five-minute Pornhub clips I've snuck a peek at once or twice when I found my way around my parents' firewall.

My best friend has been keeping serious secrets. It blows my mind Karina hangs out around this erotic mayhem and never told me. I'm utterly shocked and throbbing with curiosity about everything I see.

You're a whore just like your friend.

I give myself a shake, hoping to silent my parents' ever-present criticism and focus. I swore if I had another chance to talk to Romeo, I wouldn't embarrass myself. Yet here I am, gawking like a scared little girl.

This is the scene Romeo's used to. The kind of behavior he expects. Sexy, confident girls. Not virgins who have no idea what they're doing.

Well, some idea.

But my ex-boyfriend, Bobby, might as well have been an armadillo for all the similarity he has to Romeo.

The arrogance of having a road name like Romeo. Either he's really good in the sack or has a micro penis.

God, I hope it's not a micro penis.

The way he's staring at me and running his hand over a chin full of scruff, I think I'm about to find out.

"Did you have a good birthday?" he asks while watching me as if I'm the only person in the room.

Because he wants to get in your panties, idiot.

He doesn't even pretend he's not checking me out. His deep sapphire eyes gleam with sex and mischief while they appreciate my long, bare legs, covered by a short, frilly skirt. I practically feel the weight of his gaze as it moves up my body, over my hips, and over the swells of my breasts, barely concealed by the flimsy fabric of my camisole.

"Not really. I think you can make it better, though." Where the hell did I find the lady balls to say *that?*

Romeo likes my forwardness. A feral smile lights up his face. Hell help me, this man's insanely hot. The beard scruff doesn't hide the hard angles of his jaw. The fitted T-shirt he's wearing under his leather vest hints at the rock-hard body underneath. Tattoos peek out from every available inch of skin. His thick, dark hair seems too wild to be contained and falls over his forehead in a way that declares *badass*. Every inch of him screams reckless, gruff, crude, dirty, dangerous, and utterly irresistible.

I'm so in over my head with this guy...this man.

And I can't wait to see what happens next.

TWO

ROMEO

ATHENA HAS STARRED in a whole lot of my fantasies lately. Now she's here in the flesh, and I can't stop staring at her flawless skin and perfect body, dying for a taste. I bet her skin's soft and silky all over. Those little hands of hers will feel a whole lot better wrapped around my cock than mine do. That's for sure.

Her gaze swings from curious to scared to turned-on while she looks around the room. She's so pretty and so completely out of place in my clubhouse of sin. Too bright and clean to be somewhere so dark and dirty. I want to run my hands over every inch of her. Discover if she's as smooth as she looks. I want to paint streaks of grease from my hands all over her pristine skin, marking her as mine. It's a primitive reaction I can't explain.

Another guy might be embarrassed by the way his brothers are behaving out in the open where anyone can see. But it's a special night. This is the way we celebrate the patching in of two brothers. Two of her classmates, actually.

The Iron Bulls MC is my home and she should see what that means upfront. I ain't into sugar-coated bullshit or lies to impress anyone. Not even some chick I've been dying to bury my dick in for weeks.

Besides she must have some sort of wild in her. A little bit of bad girl dying to come out and play? Otherwise she would've run screaming from the room by now.

Melody drops off a beer for me without asking. She flicks a nasty face Athena's way and it's obvious she's about to throw some attitude next. One stern look from me and her yap snaps shut. I ask Athena what she wants to drink and ask Melody to fetch it.

Athena didn't miss the silent exchange. Her lip quivers. "Am I in the way? Is she your—"

"No." Shit, I can't see any other female in this room *but* Athena. "There's no one else."

One of her eyebrows shoots up. "Am I supposed to believe that?"

What does she want me to say? There are a lot of someone elses? Or I could be completely honest and say now that you're here, they're history?

Sure, because that's what every eighteen-year-old girl with a wild streak wants to hear.

Instead, I make a show of looking left and right. "Nope. No one here but me and you."

She seems to appreciate that and loosens up. Good. She may have come because of her friend, but I want to be the reason she stays.

"I think you know more about me than I know about you. What do you do, Romeo?"

"I own the garage and run this club."

"That's it?"

I'm not used to such genuine interest, so it takes a second to explain my specialty is working on classic cars.

"That's so cool. I always wanted a sparkly red seventy-six Corvette with Strawberry Shortcake painted on the back." Her eyes practically glow as she describes a car that's both absurd and sweet.

"Strawberry Shortcake, huh?"

Pink colors her cheeks and I can't help thinking about other parts of her that might turn pink.

"Tell me something else about you, Romeo."

"There's not much to tell, Shortcake. I'm easy to figure out."

"I doubt that—"

The need to taste something so sweet overwhelms me. I dip my head and take a kiss. My lips press against hers and I devour her mouth. She's soft and warm. At first she's tentative, then her hands slide up over my shoulders, into my hair. While I'm still trying to wrap my head around the fact that this is finally happening, she moans into my mouth.

It's not like I've never kissed a woman. I enjoy it as much as I can, using it as a means of getting where I actually want to go. But Athena? I could kiss her all night and not get tired of it.

I'm caught up in the fact that this is better than any fantasy. She's responsive and addicting. Her little whimpers and efforts to draw me closer finally snap me out of our kiss.

I can't take this girl on the couch, out in the open in

front of everyone. I don't know why, but she's special, and I want to be alone with her.

I tip my head down until our foreheads are touching and brush her cheek with my thumb. "There, now you know everything about me."

"What?" she whispers.

"I'm a man of action and take what I want how I want it. Still want to stick around?" There's no way to hide the fact that there's a lot less room in the front of my jeans. I have to push back the urge to grab her hand and rub it all over my imprisoned cock.

"Yes."

"I've wanted you since the first time I saw you."

"You have?" She's completely dazed, almost slurring her words and I haven't allowed her to have a drop of alcohol.

I can't help running the back of my hand over her cheek again. "Yeah."

She blushes and glances away. "Why? I'm pretty boring."

"I doubt that."

She shrugs and tucks her hair behind her ear. The way she's nibbling on her bottom lip's so damn cute.

"Can I show you my room?"

Can I? Seriously. I'm asking?

The corner of her mouth pulls up in a devilish smile but her bottom lip trembles, telling me she's faking whatever confidence she's trying to project. Why? Either she wants to fuck or she doesn't.

"I'd like that. It's getting too noisy to talk in here," she shouts over the music.

Not sure why it matters. The last thing we're going to do in my room is talk. *Fuck* is the only word on my mind. That's not true. *Tight young pussy* also flashes in my head.

"Is that what you want to do, Athena? Talk?" I force a smile so I don't scare her off. She's so close, I can feel the heat of her body pulsing against me. I tilt my head and brush my lips over her cheek, working my way to her ear, inhaling her scent—innocence and strawberries. "Because I had something else in mind."

"Wha—oh," she gasps, finally getting the full meaning of my words. Her breathing picks up. At least now we're on the same page.

I stand and hold my hands out to her. She lets me pull her up off the couch. I fight off the urge to toss her over my shoulder and smack her ass, claiming her as mine in front of everyone. Instead, I wrap my hand around hers— and ignore how easily we fit together. I'm not a hand-holding type of guy.

She tucks in behind me, while I weave us through the crowd and I try to not break into a sprint. There's no drunken stumble down the hallway—I hardly touched my drink. No, I want to remember every single detail about this night. Once we clear the common area, she moves to my side. She seems as eager as I am.

The walk down the hallway to my room never seemed so long.

At the door, I stop and take her in. She flashes a soul-wrecking smile at me and I can't open the door fast enough.

Inside, I flick on a small lamp. Athena presses her back

against the door. As if she just realized what's about to happen.

I'm not an asshole. She wants to go, I ain't gonna stop her, no matter how much I might want to. I'm dying to tangle our tongues together again. Strip her naked. Fill my hands with her soft skin.

Her eyes widen as I approach her with slow steps. My room's a decent size, but it's not that big, so I'm towering over her in no time. Huge eyes stare up at me and in the shadowy darkness, I can barely make out their bold, blue color. For some reason, that bugs me.

She surprises me by reaching out and touching me first. Slides her hands up over my pecs to my shoulders. I lose it, yanking her closer, but taking a gentle kiss.

At first.

The press of my mouth against hers deepens and my hands slide down into the dip of her narrow waist. My thumbs flick at the hem of her silky tank top. Underneath, her skin's warm and soft. So fucking soft.

Each kiss, she returns with equal enthusiasm. I lose a bit more control with every quick dart of her tongue against mine. I groan into her mouth and shove my hands up the sides of her ribcage until my fingers brush against the edge of her bra. I'm dying to see her in it and tug at her shirt.

I've been hard since she walked in the door, but being all pressed up against her velvety softness makes the situation behind my fly even more painful. I almost have her shirt off when she stops me.

"Wait. Romeo...I don't even know your real name."

"So?" I strip off her shirt and toss it on my dresser.

Fuck, she's fucking beautiful. The edge of my thumb brushes over one lace-covered nipple and she gasps.

Her eyes close. "I've never done this before," she whispers.

All the blood rushing to my dick must be fucking with my hearing. "What?"

"I'm a virgin."

Fuck me.

"Wish you'd mentioned that sooner, sweetheart."

She lifts her chin, defiant eyes staring up at me. "Does it matter?"

"Yeah. It matters." It matters because all of a sudden my dick's even more excited. This girl's *mine.* All fucking mine. "You want me to stop?" I ask as I brush my thumbs over her nipples again.

"You don't mind?"

She's killing me. "No, Shortcake. I don't fucking mind one bit. But I should warn you—"

Her nose wrinkles. "Warn me?"

I press one finger against her lips to keep her quiet. "I already like you. You got me thinking things I've never considered before. Giving me that pussy first might complicate things. You understand me?"

"No."

"It means, I'm not letting you go. You're in my bed from now on." I keep my gaze focused on her face, trying to read her reaction. Uncertainty lingers in her eyes.

"Is that some weird biker proposal?"

"No."

She chews on her bottom lip.

"I really want it to be you. I haven't stopped thinking about you since we met."

Her honest admission fucks me up. She says it so sweet. And there's something inside of me that's relieved this attraction hasn't been one-sided.

"You sure about this, Athena? There's no rush." Did I really just say that? My cock's ready to explode, she's offering up her pussy on a silver platter, and I'm trying to talk her out of it—why?

"I'm sure." She lifts the hem of her skirt, slowly skimming the material up then flipping it side to side, giving me glimpses of sleek, tanned thighs. I can't tell if it's nerves or playfulness responsible for the slow striptease. Doesn't matter, it's hot, whatever the reason.

Finally, she tosses the skirt on my dresser next to her shirt and stands there in a black and red lace bra and matching panties. The racy underwear contrasts with her innocent face in a way that's sexy as fuck.

"You know those are my club's colors?"

Pink spreads over her cheeks. "I…well…uh," she stammers out the words and it clicks.

"You wore this for me?" It's such a sweet, girlish thing to do and because I'm a perverted old fuck, it gets me even harder.

"Turn around." My mouth's so dry I have to force the words out.

Not one of my fantasies touched on how perfect she is in the flesh.

I'm breathing so heavy, I probably sound like a fucking dragon bearing down on her. I've never been this turned on. Not since my own first time. Many years and many women ago. Taking it slow and gentle is testing all my willpower.

I have to get my hands on her. When our bodies touch, she jumps and turns to look up at me with huge eyes. I settle my hands on her shoulders, softly stroking warm, satin skin. "Tell me what you've done before?"

"What? What do you mean?"

What I'm trying to figure out is how a girl this hot is still a virgin. Is she one of those virgin-whores who's taken it in every hole except her pussy, thinking somehow that keeps her chaste? Or is she really as innocent as she's acting?

Leaning over, I put my mouth against her ear. My thumb strokes over her bottom lip. "What I mean is, have you sucked cock? Has anyone licked your cunt? Stuff like that, sweetheart."

Her eyes widen at my crude words and it only fires me up more.

"I, uh, I…"

She can't form any words because my fingers slipped inside her panties to gently stroke her. Haven't even touched her clit yet and she's already panting. My other hand works her bra loose, setting free perky little tits. Tits begging to be held in my big hands so I can work my thumbs over her nipples until she's thrashing against me.

"Reed," I whisper in her ear.

"What?"

"You asked what my real name is. It's Reed. That's what I want you screamin' out when I fuck you."

"Oh, oh, o-kay." Her lips form a shaky smile. "I like that."

"Good." Can't remember the last woman I bothered telling my name. Honestly, I can't remember the last one who asked. I'm not in the habit of keeping them around long enough to get curious about things like names.

"You ever come before?"

"I, think so."

"That's a no." Good, now I've got a plan. I need to get her off first. Because I'm ninety-nine percent certain it'll be game over about two seconds after I squeeze my dick in her. Her body's trembling underneath my fingers. I'm a sick fucker, because I like her on edge. Her fear feeds my inner animal who's ready to claim every perfect inch of her. I need to speed this up.

Dipping back inside her panties, I run my fingers over her pussy lips, then up through her slit, stopping to spread her wetness over her clit. Even though I'm barely touching her, she hisses in a soft breath and wraps her fingers around my arm.

"That's it, little one. Relax, I got you." Her body melts into mine as I keep stroking and teasing her. Working her up until her hips jerk and chase my hand.

"Oh, oh, oh…"

"Yeah. That feel good?"

"Y..yes."

Inside I'm flippin' out, but outside, I'm taking things nice and slow. My patience is rewarded a few minutes later when she comes, gasping and quivering on my hand.

"Beautiful."

Her big eyes flutter open and stare up at me. "Wow."

Wow is fuckin' right and I think it's the first time I've ever used that word.

"Leave those panties on and get up in my bed."

She's too nervous to be seductive about it, and it's hotter than fuck the way she tiptoes to my bed and carefully sits on the edge.

As I stalk over to her, I catch her bottom lip trembling again.

Even though I'm a first class bastard, I have to stop and ask, "You sure you want this, Athena?"

"Yes. I really, really do."

She reaches out, and grabs my belt. Perfect, white teeth sink into her bottom lip while she works my jeans open.

"Lie back." There's a good chance if she keeps undressing me in her nervous, awkward way, I'll explode right in her face. And that's not how I want her first time to go down. I probably look ridiculous shedding clothes as fast as possible, but I don't give a fuck.

She scoots into the middle of the bed, still watching every move I make. In seconds, I'm climbing in after her, parting her legs and crawling up her body to bury my face against her pussy. She smells and tastes like water after crawling through the desert. Soft moans drag from her throat and she arches her back, shoving her cunt in my face.

"Want me to lick you?"

"Uh...if you want to?" She sits up and this time the fear in her eyes doesn't excite me.

"Don't worry, little one, I plan to put my mouth on every single part of you tonight."

"Oh," she whispers.

Tonight. Not now. I'd love to spend some time getting her off with my mouth, but I don't think I can wait much longer. We've got all night. And tomorrow and the next day. Because fuck if I'm ever letting her out of my sight. No fucking way.

I kiss my way up her body until we're nose to nose. She's unbelievably pretty up close. My dick likes her too, because he's pushing up against her lace-covered pussy like one pushy bastard. Fuck if she's not grinding against it trying to find release. I take a second, which my cock's not thrilled about, to run my thumbs over her cheeks. "You okay?"

Her hands grip my biceps, sliding to my shoulders and over my back. Every stroke of her fingers against me burns like a lick of fire. "Yes," she finally answers.

Almost forgot. I reach over and drag a condom out of my nightstand and roll it on. "You know it's probably gonna hurt the first time?"

She scrunches up her nose. "Yeah." Her lush mouth curls up in a teasing smile. "Would you please fuck me already?"

A growl rips out of my throat, and I take her sassy mouth in a fierce kiss. My hand skims the length of her body and shoves her panties to the side. She breaks our kiss, blinking up at me. "Do you want me to take them off?"

"No. I'm going to keep them as a fuckin' trophy."

She blinks.

I'm not kidding.

My cock lines up and I sink into her slowly. The tip of my dick's barely inside and already she's tense, making it impossible to make any more progress. My lips find her forehead. "Relax, Shortcake. I'm trying to be gentle."

A tight smile plays over her lips. "I know."

Christ, I need to be inside her more than I need to breathe. Even if I have to fight my way in. I hold her gaze the entire time. Watch the pain flicker over her face. Underneath me she sighs and wriggles, spreading her legs wider.

"Good girl. Spread those legs and take me," I whisper.

A few more strokes and I'm balls-deep. I have to take a second and catch my breath. So motherfuckin' tight. I'm struggling to suck in air and not shoot my load at the same time.

"Oh. Oh, Reed."

I can't stop myself from checking out where my cock's buried in her pussy. I slide back and stare at the smear of blood on the condom. Fuck. It might be sick, but it's the hottest thing I've ever seen. My thumbs brush over her cheeks and I stare into her eyes again. "You okay?"

"Yes. It's starting to… It feels better."

I thrust back in, even though her pussy's got me in a death grip. Her eyes roll back in her head and she turns her face to the side. My lips find her neck, biting and kissing a path to her mouth as I keep fucking her slow and steady. Not coming is a struggle I don't mind. When I look into her eyes again they're shiny.

"You want me to stop?" Christ, I hope she says no, because I don't think I could stop if my life depended on it.

"No. Harder. More. Please."

The look on her face is saying anything *but* harder. But it's what she asked for, so I give it to her. She grunts and takes it. "Let me in, baby. I know how bad you want it, just relax and let me in."

Finally she loosens up a little and a few strokes later she seems happier. Her hips jerk up and her moans grow louder.

"That's it. Good girl. You gonna come with my cock buried in you?"

"I don't know. I want something. I…I…"

She trails off, because I bend down to suck one of her nipples into my mouth, and one of my hands reaches between us to stroke her clit. She tightens and thrashes under me. "Fuck, Reed! Right there."

Thank fuck, now I can plow into her. She keeps yelling, and I fuck her like she's the last fuck I'll ever have, grabbing her hips and slamming myself inside her over and over until her pussy clenches around my dick.

She's flushed and sweaty, tears rolling down her cheeks, but it's the smile on her face that makes me lose it.

Maybe I'm lightheaded from the load I just poured into the condom, but the emptiness I usually carry in my chest is gone. Replaced by this girl. Strangely, I want the feeling to last.

Athena

That was *so* worth waiting for.

I'm *so* glad I never did it with Bobby.

Both are probably inappropriate thoughts with Romeo still inside me, but I can't help it.

He brushes the hair off my forehead—a sweetly tender

gesture made even sweeter when he presses his lips there. "Are you okay?" he asks.

The hot, demanding, growly biker I've known for a few weeks, who soaked my panties every time I got within ten feet of him? Turns out he's hard on the outside but sweet and gentle on the inside. *This* guy makes my heart want to jump out of my chest and into his hands.

And that's not what I want out of this.

I'm not stupid. There's no way this ends in some fairy tale where the hard, older biker, and the young, virgin ride off into the sunset together. We're not making babies —*gross*—nor are we going to play house together—*double yuck*. It may have worked out that way for my best friend, Karina. The kind of lightning she and Dante have won't strike this clubhouse twice.

Not a problem. I don't want that anyway. I'm leaving for Los Angeles tomorrow. No man—no matter how hot he is, no matter that he just took my virginity and is staring down at me in a way that says he's got no intention of letting me leave his bed, is going to stop me.

At least he's given me some very pleasant memories to take with me to California.

"Athena, did I hurt you?"

I wriggle a bit and take a deep breath—or try to. "No. But you're crushing me a little."

He chuckles and rolls to the side. "Be right back."

When he returns, he's naked and I'm torn between trying not to stare and trying to count the ridges of his abs. The sheet I'd pulled up to my chin is ripped away by his free hand as he settles on the edge of the bed. Without asking or hesitating, he parts my legs and wipes me down gently with a warm washcloth.

I'm too mortified at the intimate, matter-of-fact way he performs the simple act to move or speak.

"You're the prettiest shade of red right now," he says in a low, gravely voice that makes my insides shiver.

I dare to glance up and find him staring at my face. We stare at each other for a few seconds before he takes the washcloth back into the bathroom. When he returns, he yanks the sheet I had burrowed back under off me again. "Stop trying to hide yourself from me," he growls, climbing on top of me. He settles himself over me, his weight barely brushing against my body. Hands. Where should I put my hands?

His arms. The rolling muscles of his biceps, the colorful ink decorating every inch of skin. Good Lord, he's my own personal arm porn. My hands brush against him, then squeeze, marveling at how hard he is.

"Christ girl, you keep staring at my arms that way, and I'm gonna have to fuck you again. Not sure you can handle it."

"I can handle you," I whisper, even though I'm not quite sure that's true.

He drops his head, pressing his lips to mine. I've never been kissed by a *man.* Only boys my own age and they clearly didn't know what they were doing. Kissing Romeo is better than almost going all the way with Bobby.

His bristly five-o-clock shadow rasps against my skin. I've been wondering what it would feel like to kiss Romeo since the day we met. Now I know. It's as if he's conquering me, permanently ruining my mind, soul, and mouth for any other man. I try kissing him back, but I'm lost in the way his tongue caresses mine, the way his stubble scrapes against my skin, his erection digging into my thigh. I let my legs fall open, inviting him in once again.

When he finally pulls back, he's breathing hard. Dark eyes stare back at me, burning with need.

"You sure you can take me again?" he asks, glancing down at his rapidly growing erection.

"Wow," I mutter.

"I like that," he says as he presses his lips to mine again. He keeps kissing me, invading my mouth and thoughts. I'm swirling so deep, I barely register the shift of his body or the ripping of a wrapper. I do notice the nudge of his cock against my entrance again, so I spread my legs wider and lift my hips, letting him slide right in. He groans into my mouth and I swallow down the beautiful sound of making this man lose control.

We're both breathing hard when we part. "I gotta see you, baby." It's the only warning I get before he rolls us to the side. Somehow his cock slips free, but he settles me on top of him. "Lift up."

Confused, it takes a second to figure out what he wants. I rise up on my knees, and he settles one hand on my shoulder, keeping me where he wants. His other hand fists his cock, holding himself steady so I can sink down.

"Oh my God," I gasp and try to raise myself, but his hand on my shoulder keeps me in place.

"Take it for me, Athena. You can do it."

"Oh. *Ow*. Oh."

He chuckles at the silly sounds that keep popping out

of my mouth. Once I've got the hang of it, he cups my hips and urges me up and down. My head falls back and my eyes close. His hands slide up my rib cage, stopping below my breasts and I realize how exposed I am up here. My head snaps up, eyes open. I cross my arms over my chest, slowing my movements. Romeo's forehead slashes into a frown.

"What're you doing?"

"I don't…I'm all flat compared to—"

He smacks my hands away. "What'd I tell you? Don't fuckin' hide yourself from me." His hands roughly close over my breasts, squeezing and tweaking my nipples. "These are fuckin' beautiful. Fit my hands just right. Knock your shit off and ride my dick."

I'm not used to so many crude commands. Hell, I'm not used to any of this. My brain might be insulted, but my body loves it. Heat races over my skin and my pussy throbs with pleasure.

"That's better," he growls, dragging his hands away from my tits and back to my hips.

"Reed…oh…Reed."

"That's it."

"Oh my…oh shit. So good."

He groans in agreement and when I glance down, his eyes are screwed shut. "Are you okay?" Crap. Am I hurting him? Doing it too hard?

"I'm trying not to blow until you come, sweetheart."

Oh. *Oh.* "I…I," I stutter, close to something happening.

He lifts me off him, tossing me to the side. "Reed!"

"Hands and knees. Don't fuck around."

I'm mortified. Especially when he grabs my hips,

yanking me into the position he wants, leaving me so exposed. Then I'm gasping in pleasure as he pushes back inside. "Am I hurting you?"

It's *different*. But it doesn't hurt. "No."

The first few strokes are gentle and feel amazing. He zaps nerves I didn't know I had to life. After he lets me get used to the new position, he moves faster. Harder. Deep strokes until he's pounding into me so hard, I can't keep myself up. "Ow."

"Too much?"

"Yes."

He grunts and pulls out. Grabs me and flips me onto my back, and before I know what's happening, he's back inside. We both groan as he pushes in as deep as he can, then slowly swivels his hips grinding himself into my clit.

"Oh, Romeo, Reed, right there. That's…" My words evaporate as my muscles finally spasm around him.

"Fuck, Athena." He grinds into me harder. Relentlessly. Until he thrusts once more and comes with a satisfied, growly noise that makes me feel like an A-list porn star.

"You're gonna kill me. I'm too old to work that hard," Romeo says with a lazy smirk.

"Sorry."

He leans over and presses a kiss to my forehead then leaves to clean himself up. I sit and gather my clothes. He probably wants me to leave. I can be dignified about this, right? No way am I planning to be some clingy chick who overstays her welcome. One and done.

The corners of my mouth lift. Or two and done.

Romeo steps out of the bathroom and the fierce

expression on his face makes me reconsider. "Where're you going?"

"I…uh. Well, I figured you didn't want me to stay over. You don't have to worry. I'm not gonna be like, some virgin clinger or something now that you deflowered me."

In three, maybe four steps, he crosses the room and yanks my clothes out of my hands. "Were you listening before?"

"What?"

"I ain't letting you go. You climbed into my bed willingly, gave me that sweet pussy. You're not leaving."

My dream of moving to California keeps beating at the edge of my mind. "Are you serious?"

"Fuck yeah."

"What about—"

"Athena, I'm tired. You're staying. Can we do this tomorrow?" He stalks over to his dresser and tosses a T-shirt at me. "Put this on so you don't wake up with my mouth on your tits."

"I might like that."

"You're my sassy little bitch, aren't you?"

My jaw drops. "Did you just call me a bitch?"

His mouth twists into one of those sexy smirks that make my girly parts tingle.

"Fuck yeah, I did," he says, completely unapologetic. "Now. We're clear. You're staying."

Instead of words, I nod, although I don't know why I bother. He didn't *ask*.

Once we're settled in bed, my head's resting on his chest but my mind won't settle down.

I feel like I just made a promise I can't keep.

THREE

ROMEO

WAKING with the soft weight of a woman in my bed isn't a regular occurrence for me, believe it or not. Athena wasn't wrong last night. Usually, I prefer to sleep alone. Hell, half the time girls don't even make it through my bedroom door.

I like my space.

Makes it even funnier that the one girl I actually *want* to spend the night, was ready to jet about five seconds after I pulled my dick out of her.

The sensation of being used as her personal body pillow doesn't fill me with dread.

Interesting.

Hooking my finger in a tangle of blonde curls, I push her hair off her face so I can get a better look at her. No raccoon eyes or smeared makeup. A fresh-faced sleeping beauty.

What the fuck am I doing with a girl half my age?

Before I have a chance to give it any more thought, Athena stirs. Her breathing changes. Her lashes tickle my skin. Finally, she picks her head up off my chest and blinks a few times.

"Are you staring at me?"

"Yeah. You're a pretty girl." Prettiest girl I've woken up with in a long time. But I keep that to myself, because I doubt she'll find it flattering.

Her eyes widen like no one's ever paid her a compliment before. How is that even possible?

I can't help stroking my finger across her cheek. "How do you feel?"

"Happy," she says without thinking it over.

I don't know what I expected her to say. The directness of that one word has a simple innocence to it. I want her to wake up happy every day. I want to *be* the one who makes her wake up happy every day.

"I meant, are you sore?"

"Oh." She wrinkles her nose and shifts, which stirs my dick to life—not that he hadn't been on alert as it was. "A little."

My thumb traces over her bottom lip. "We can do other things today."

She nips my finger. "That's right. You promised to put your mouth all over me last night and never got to it."

Honest to God laughter rumbles out of me. She grins and pushes herself up, accidentally brushing her hand over my cock.

"Oh." Curious eyes stare at me. "Morning wood's a real thing, huh? Not a myth?"

"No myth." I really wish I hadn't bothered to give her the T-shirt to sleep in last night. Feeling her warm, satin skin up against me would have made this morning perfect. Tonight she gets no clothes.

I reach down to pull her to me for a kiss, but she shies away. Pink colors her cheeks. "I need to pee."

Shit, she makes me laugh. "Go. Me and my morning wood will be waiting for you."

"Cocky motherfucker," she mumbles as she crawls over me. It only makes me laugh harder.

Couple minutes later she's standing in my doorway with a face full of confusion and maybe hurt. "Why do you have a girl's T-shirt on your floor in here?"

Here's my punishment for being such a slob.

Okay, maybe I don't encourage a lot of chicks into my personal space. Doesn't mean some haven't spent time in here. But after last night, only girl in here is Athena. That I know for certain.

"It's B.A."

"What the hell does that mean?"

"Before Athena," I explain and run my gaze over her to see if she's buying it.

"Eww. Tell me you didn't fuck someone yesterday before I got here."

I actually have to think about it. "No."

"So you're just a pig who doesn't clean up after himself?"

"Pretty much."

She grumbles and tosses the shirt back in the bathroom. Then strolls to the side of the bed and stares down at me. "Are you planning to feed me?"

"Yeah, my cock."

Her jaw drops in a cute, shocked way that's so hot, it

makes me want to say more obnoxious things. "Did you really just say that?"

"Yup." There's no point in hiding who I really am if I want her to stick around.

Her mouth twists into a smirk, and I think she's trying not to laugh. I reach out and run my fingers up her bare thigh, up under her shirt to her hip. "Well, at least you're direct."

"Got no time for bullshit."

"Will you teach me how you like it done?"

I assume she means I need to teach her how to give a blowjob, which is fine by me. "Fuck, yeah."

Her stomach rumbles and I get a prick of something. A conscience? Concern for someone other than my dick? That's new. Throwing off the sheet, I sit up and pull her to me. Her arms settle around my neck and she tips her head down. "Guess you're hungry?"

She nods so vigorously, it makes me laugh. "I think I'll be a more attentive student if I'm not lightheaded from hunger."

Christ, she's cute. "Give me a second."

When I return from the bathroom, she's wearing her skirt from last night and my T-shirt. Except, now she's tied it in a knot at her hip. "Cute."

Her smile's bright and beautiful. I could compliment her all day long if that face were the reward. The way she watches me pull on jeans and a shirt has me wanting to say fuck it to the food but I keep it together.

My cock doesn't control me, as much as it thinks otherwise.

Athena

Weird. In my head, I imagined hanging out at the Iron Bulls MC clubhouse would be fun and exciting. Decadent and dirty. And it was. Last night. This morning, it's a bunch of hungover half-dressed people.

As soon as we enter the main room, one of Romeo's club brothers calls him over and he drags me along.

"Everything good?" he asks the guy whose leather vest reads "Nero."

Nero glances at me and I'm about to take that as my cue to get lost when Romeo pulls me into his lap. His arm bands around my waist keeping me tethered to his body. Nero raises an eyebrow before continuing the conversation.

"Yeah. No trouble. All clear."

Romeo nods as if the vague words have some meaning to him. The nod seems to also dismiss Nero and he ambles away without saying anything else.

"Is there a reason you didn't introduce me to your friend?"

Romeo stares at me, and I wonder if I offended him or pissed him off.

I don't get to find out, because Dante and Karina join us. She gives me a pointed stare and I grin back at her. Throwing a thumbs up would probably be childish so I contain myself. Barely.

"There should be breakfast in the kitchen, Shortcake," Romeo says, giving me a nudge off his lap.

"Do you want anything?"

That sexy smirk that makes me want to rip my clothes

off and drag him into the nearest private room twists his mouth. "You know what I want."

I can't help but lean over and kiss his cheek which seems to surprise him. "Bring back coffee?" he asks.

"You got it."

Karina points to the kitchen doors and follows me inside.

As soon as the double doors stop flapping behind us, she grabs my hand. "Are you okay?"

"Oh, yeah."

Her gaze slides to the kitchen doors and she waves a jerky hand in the air. "Romeo? Really?"

"Why not? You've got a sexy-ass biker, why can't I have one?"

She rolls her eyes. "He's not a Ken doll."

"You're telling *me*. Ken wishes he had a—"

"Stop right there. I don't want to know anything about Romeo's package."

I grin like a fool, because my best friend knows exactly how my mind works and what words were about to jump off my tongue. Her face softens. "He seems to really like you. I've never seen him so…nice before."

"Really?"

Instead of answering, she frowns. "Does he know you're leaving for California?"

"Well, we didn't really do a lot of talking."

"Ew."

I snort. "Why are you being such a prude?"

"I'm not." She hesitates. Bites her lip. I know my friend well enough to know something's bothering her. "What's wrong, Karina?"

"Dante work you over good last night?" one of the girls asks. She looks familiar and I'm about to ask her name, when Karina answers.

"Mind your own business, Melody."

The girl stomps out of the kitchen and Karina pulls me over to a table in the corner.

"Didn't she go to our high school?"

"Yeah. Ignore her. She likes to start trouble."

"Does she—"

"Yes."

"Has she—"

"Probably."

Now I'm the one saying, "Ew."

"Can we talk for a sec before you get all wrapped up with Romeo?"

"Yeah. Sure. What's wrong?"

She jumps up and grabs a loaf of bread, butter, jars of peanut butter and jelly, a knife, and returns.

"Milk?"

She sniffs the carton in the fridge before bringing it over and setting it on the table with two glasses.

I don't know much about the Iron Bulls or bikers or hell, men in general really, but I'm starting to get a sense of things. "So, Romeo's probably banged every chick I see in this clubhouse?"

She shudders and I'm struck with what an awkward question that is for her. Dante's probably screwed all those girls, too. "How can you stand that?"

"I trust Dante."

Why? He could do whatever he wants while she's away

at school or whatever. How would she ever know the difference?

"I hope you're still practicing safe sex."

She gives me a sharp glare and thrusts the butter knife in her hand at me. "Here, butter your own bread."

That's fine, she never uses enough butter anyway.

"What'd you want to talk about?" I ask when she looks a little less pissed.

"Promise not to judge me?"

Oh, shit. I really hope she's not pregnant.

"I won't. Spill."

She fiddles with her sandwich and won't meet my eyes. "I found out I have a sister."

"Holy shit. When? How?"

"My father's a two-timing pig."

This doesn't surprise me.

"Well, what's she like?"

"I don't know yet. Dante's going to get her number from my father."

"Wait, why Dante?"

"He had a talk with my father."

I almost choke on my sandwich as I picture big scary Dante *talking* to Karina's weasel of a father. It makes me like Dante even more. I kind of hope his massive fists were a part of their conversation. While my parents kept me in line with a constant stream of criticism and insults, Karina's father's parenting style can only be described as absent.

"Do you think you can stick around to go with me to meet her?" Karina asks.

Crapcrapcrap. I can't say no to my best friend. But I'm

also afraid the longer I stay here with Romeo, the harder it will be to leave.

I have to follow my dream. I *have* to. I'll die if I repeat my mother's mistakes. Never leaving the small town where I grew up. Marrying the first man who paid me any attention. Or worse, falling in love with a big, bad biker and then getting my ass kicked to the curb when he's bored with me. Giving Romeo the power to hurt me that way goes against everything inside me. I might as well slit my wrists now if I'm going to throw my life away.

I almost regret not listening to my parents about applying to college.

"Athena?" Karina's soft voice pulls me out of the life-choices-freak-out I'm having.

Calm down. You've got a plan.

"I have to be there by the twenty-fifth. I'm signed up for a class."

She raises an eyebrow. "Really?"

Heat floods my cheeks and I duck my head. "An acting class. It's supposed to be a good way to network and get auditions."

"That's good. So you have a plan?"

"Sort of."

She nods as if that makes her happy.

"I'll be back for Fourth of July."

"Okay." She rolls her bottom lip and chews on it for a second. "Shit. I don't know what I'm going to do without you around."

"You've got Dante to keep you busy."

She gives me a sad smile. "Yes. But it's not the same."

FOUR

ROMEO

I HATE LETTING Athena out of my sight for more than the few minutes I allow her to go to the bathroom in private. When the girls return from the kitchen—finally—I pull her into my lap and kiss her cheek.

While we were waiting, Dante went outside to talk to Karina's father. When I explain that to Karina, she heads back upstairs.

Athena nuzzles against my neck, kissing along my jaw. "You smell like peanut butter."

"We ate peanut butter and jelly sandwiches."

"Where's mine?" I tease her.

An apologetic expression turns her mouth down. "I'm sorry. I'll go get—"

I tighten my hold on her. "I'm kidding. I'd rather smear it all over you and lick it off your body anyway."

She shivers against me and I'm ready to take her back upstairs right the fuck now.

The sharp bite of desire for a woman usually goes

away after I fuck her. Not this time. The blistering want burns through me *worse* than before I got her underneath me. I'm seriously fucked here.

Even more awkward, it's not enough to have her near me. No, I gotta have her right in my motherfuckin' lap where the soft weight of her body presses into me in all the right spots.

This is new. Everyone in the clubhouse senses it.

Clubwhores keep glaring at Athena because they know damn well I don't act this way. Part of me feels a bit shitty about that. A very small part. But still.

My brothers are dying to razz my ass. Fuck knows I've got it coming.

Maybe I should get the fuck out of here. Once I get out on the road, it'll clear my head.

Except for the part where I want Athena with me on the back of my bike.

"Anyone want to hit up the music fest over in Red Rock?" Sadie asks as Dante and Karina return.

Dante groans. "Is it gonna be a bunch of bands where all the boys are wearin' nut-huggers and screaming about how their mommies didn't love them enough?"

Karina giggles and Dante uses it as an excuse to grope her tits.

Athena turns to me with a hopeful expression. "Can we go? I love Attila and they're on that tour."

One glance at Dante and it's obvious this is the last thing he wants to do. "Yeah, Shortcake."

Karina wriggles out of Dante's hold and grabs Athena's hand. "We'll be back."

I try really hard not to laugh until the girls leave.

"I'll go see who else wants to go," Sadie offers.

"Thanks, Sadie-girl."

She winks at me before leaving.

"Really?" Dante groans.

"Come on. You saw how excited the girls were."

"You know it's gonna be a bunch of screaming girls, pansy-assed boys in skinny jeans, shitty music, and ten dollar beers, right?"

"Never knew you were so anti-social, brother."

He cocks his head. The *really, motherfucker?* expression he's wearing cements my decision.

"It's gonna be crowded," he warns.

"Good thing I'll have my enforcer with me."

"Dick," he snarls before stomping off.

Sometimes it's fun to be president.

ATHENA AND KARINA return from the parking lot. Athena's clutching a pair of jeans to her chest and carrying a pair of sneakers.

"What's that?"

"Just grabbed a few things from my car."

"You got a bag or something?"

Her eyes widen. "Yeah, but I didn't think you'd want—"

I stand and set my hands on her shoulders, staring her right in the eyes. "Bring in whatever you want and put it up in my room."

"Are you sure?"

It seems she's confused or reluctant. I don't know her well enough yet to be sure. We walk outside together and I wait while she pulls a backpack out of her car. She's got some boxes and other bags in there as well.

"Taking a trip?"

She slams her trunk shut and spins around. "No. It's just stuff I cleaned out of my locker at school."

Seems she must have had a big locker to fit so much in. "You want to bring more inside?"

"No. This is enough."

I hoist her bag on my shoulder and lead her back inside, where she and Karina disappear upstairs.

Sadie rounds up a bunch of brothers and their ladies. The girls take so long to return, I start wondering if they changed their minds. We're waiting outside when they finally burst through the door. Athena walks over shyly.

"Karina said I should wear this. Is that okay?"

Fuck yeah, it is. Looks like I owe Karina a big fuckin' thank you. She found my girl a thin, red Iron Bulls tank top to wear.

"You look good in my club's colors."

She blushes and glances at her feet. "Thanks."

"You need to stop by your house and pick up more clothes or anything else?" I hope she's reading the *you're never leaving my bed* intent behind my words.

Panic flashes over her face. "No. My parents—no. That wouldn't be a good idea. They think Karina and I are out of town."

I guess I can't blame her. The uptight couple I met at her graduation probably wouldn't be real receptive to their little princess showing up on the back of a motorcycle driven by a man twice her age.

She glances at the bike and bites her lower lip. "I've never ridden on a motorcycle before."

"It's easy, Shortcake. I'll do all the hard stuff."

A naughty grin lights up her face.

"We going or what?" Whip, the MC's Road Captain, barks out.

"Calm the fuck down," I snap.

Athena's eyes widen at my tone and the way everyone responds to it, but I ignore her reaction. She'll get used to things around here in time.

I walk her through the basics of being a good passenger, but before I'm finished the guys start up their hogs, drowning out the last of my words. Athena nods vigorously to show me she understands and lets me strap her into a helmet.

Fuck, if she doesn't feel perfect up against me.

She doesn't loosen her grip around my waist once, and each time I shout over the wind to ask if she's okay, she yells back, "Yes."

When we make it to the concert grounds, she hops off before I even shut the bike down.

"Oh my God, that was so much fun!"

She has trouble pulling off the helmet, but that's fine. I like having an excuse to touch her. Karina runs over and they do their girly hugging and high-pitched chatter thing. Dante glances at me and shrugs.

Because I insist on paying for our little group of eleven, my wallet gets raped at the ticket window. Once

Athena grabs my hand and drags me to the security checkpoint, I forget all about it. Security doesn't seem to like the looks of us and we are all but cavity searched. Thankfully, none of us are carrying today.

Wretched noise echoes over the grassy knolls. There are two stages set up on opposite ends of the park. It's hard to tell which one has the crappier bands since every note spewing from the dozens of speakers sounds like shit. I raise an eyebrow at Dante who laughs. "Told ya."

"You'll recognize the headliner," Sadie assures me.

"Yeah, when do they go on stage?"

"About seven hours from now."

"Fuck me."

Athena

This is the weirdest group date—if you count the other two girls from the MC who joined us—I've ever been on. Karina and I have come to this festival the last two summers, so we know what to expect. The crowds don't bother us. Although Dante and Romeo look like they want to murder everyone in their path, it is pretty funny to watch the way people can't scatter out of our way fast enough.

After we decide which bands we want to see, we stake out a spot where we have a decent view of the big screens.

Karina glances at me and a sly smile turns her mouth up.

"What?" Dante asks.

"Karina and I usually go hang in the mosh pit," I answer.

Romeo looks at me like I'm nuts.

"Sweetheart, we go down there and someone looks at you the wrong way, let alone slams into you, I'll fuckin' kill 'em."

Dante seems to have a similar opinion. Karina shrugs and cuddles up with her man. I get the feeling whatever he says goes.

I'm not so sure how I feel about being told what to do.

Dante tosses a blanket at us from the backpack he carried in and spreads out his own before motioning Karina back into his arms. They're all lovey-dovey and generally disgusting.

Romeo chuckles when I turn away and gag. He pulls me down between his outstretched legs. "You've seen this band before?"

"Oh, yeah. We met the singer last year. He was super cool to us—" I realize I'm babbling and probably boring the hell out of Romeo.

He raises one dark eyebrow at me. "And?"

"I'm sure you don't want to hear about my silly escapades." He slides his hand into my hair and I shy away. "I'm all sweaty."

"So?" This time he yanks me to him. "Don't pull away from me. We got more than a little sweaty last night."

My jaw drops and I let a little "Oh" sound out. He takes my surprise as an invitation to press his lips against mine hard, but quick. "Plan to get sweaty with you later," he says as he pulls away.

I have no words.

It's impossible to concentrate on anything other than the hard man wrapped around me. Last year, I was right down by the stage in the thick of it. Karina and I were trying to figure out how to talk our way backstage to meet a few of the band guys.

This year, all I can think about is last night with Romeo. What tonight might bring. More than once, I almost turn and ask him if we can leave.

As darkness falls, the air cools off enough that I'm uncomfortable. Romeo pulls me tighter. "You okay?"

I bob my head up and down because the heat pouring off him has a different effect on me than I think he intended. He sweeps my hair to the side and dips his head down, running his nose along my neck. My breathing picks up and I let out a small moan. Thoughts of what I want him to do to me are making me dizzy.

"Are you okay?" he asks again.

"Yes."

One of his hands slips under my tank top, strokes over my belly, and stops at my breasts.

"Romeo?"

He keeps his mouth at my ear while his thumb flicks over my nipple. "I want to suck on your tits."

"Now? Here?"

"Right now." His low, gritty voice seeps inside my body. I don't hear the words as much as I feel them. My nipples are especially responsive to his desires and don't care that we're in a crowd full of people.

Any shyness I had disappears around Romeo. I shift my body so my hand can brush over the crotch of his jeans. "Oh, wow."

"I ain't fucking around, Shortcake."

"I never got to kiss you here," I whisper in his ear as I

rub my hand a little harder over his erection. He hisses in a breath and pinches my nipple until I gasp. Not a bad gasp though.

"You're gonna do more than kiss my cock, sweetheart."

"Oh, yeah?"

He slides his hand back down and pops the button of my jeans open. Even so, they're too tight to fit his hand inside and he growls in frustration. "Lean back."

"I can't. There are people everywhere. Someone will see."

"It's dark. No one's paying attention to us. I need to feel how wet you are."

I lean back and he eases the zipper down, then shoves his hand in my panties. "Fuck me. This shitty music get you horny?"

"No. You do."

He sucks and nips at my neck until I'm moaning, and despite what he said, I think anyone could look over and figure out exactly what we're doing.

I'm strangely turned on by the idea of someone watching. Even better, what if one of the cameras scanning the crowd caught us and beamed the image of Romeo with one hand down my pants and one under my shirt to the entire place?

He slides one finger inside me, working me slow but steady enough that I'm ready to explode after a few minutes.

"Oh, oh, oh."

"Shhh, not too loud."

"I can't—" He keeps easing in and out of me with the

right amount of pressure until I let loose, pulsing in pleasure around his finger.

He kisses my cheek and while I'm catching my breath, fixes my jeans. "That was beautiful."

"I think it's your turn."

FIVE

ROMEO

I'VE DONE a lot of crazy shit in my life.

Nothing compares to getting Athena off in the middle of a crowd. And I've fucked plenty of bitches out in the open. Especially at the clubhouse.

"You know this place better than I do. Where can we go?" I whisper in her ear.

I don't have to explain any better than that. She jumps up and holds her hand out to me.

Dante snickers as we leave, and I give him the finger.

We sneak behind a few of the concession stands, and as soon as we come across a hard surface, I've got her pinned up against it. Lucky for us, it's a brick wall. She's kissing me back just as hungry and fierce, even helps me work my belt loose and free my crushed cock.

No condoms.

Fuck.

We passed half a dozen booths today where they were handing condoms out by the bucketful and it never occurred to me to grab one.

Idiot.

"You on the pill, Athena?"

Well, that's a spell-breaker. Her lower lip trembles and she shakes her head. "No. Please don't—"

"Stop. I won't."

She wraps her hand around me, sliding it gently up and down. Fuck, I've wanted her hands and mouth wrapped around my dick for-fucking-ever. Slowly, she sinks to her knees. With the shitty lighting and pressure of possibly getting caught at any moment, I don't get to fully enjoy the sight of her kneeling in front of me. I *do* let loose with a string of curses when she licks the head of my dick, all soft and sweet.

"I'm not sure I'm any good at this," she whispers.

"It's kind of hard to fuck it up. Unless you gnaw on it or something."

She snorts, the air drifting over my dick, working me up even more.

"Suck it, sweetheart."

It's shadowy and dark back here, but there's enough light to see her staring up at me and licking her lips. The second she takes the head of my dick in her mouth, I groan.

"Good girl," I whisper, and she smiles around my cock.

I'm one lucky fucking bastard.

Athena takes her time, teasing me, swirling her tongue around the head, then tracing her tongue down my cock. Fire shoots through my veins and I shift my hips, pushing all the way in her hot little mouth. Love the kissing and licking thing she's doing, but I've decided I need to get her home and fuck her properly.

My fingers work into her hair, holding it out of her way and holding her still for me to work myself in deep. She drops her hands and opens her mouth wider, letting me rock into her mouth at my pace.

A pace that's hard, but she takes it like a champ, gagging a few times, but hanging in there. She braces her hands on my thighs, holding on for dear life.

"Ready?"

She makes a rough sound in the back of her throat that travels right to my balls and trips my switch. At the last second, it registers that noise sounded like, *No*. It's too late though, one second I'm shooting in her hot wet mouth, the next she's shaking out of my grasp, coughing and spitting, while I'm still shooting cum on her face. Not quite how I expected that to end.

"Shit," she sputters, spits, and curses.

This might be a first.

"Are you okay, Athena?"

She spits again, which honestly is getting to be a little insulting.

"I think I got cum up my nose."

I can't help it. She looks so fucking flustered, lost, disgusted, so many things—I start laughing.

"Don't laugh at me, you jerk," her little hand smacks my thigh as I'm busy tucking myself away.

"Come here." What I *should* be pissed about—the crappy ending—doesn't seem as important as making sure she's okay.

I help her up and use the edge of my shirt to wipe her face clean. Even in the weak lighting, her red cheeks stand out. "I've never done that before."

"Given head? Or—"

"Had someone come in my *mouth.*"

For some ridiculous reason, I'm pissed she's got *any* experience in this area. The chicks I'm used to know how to suck and swallow like fucking Hoovers. Still, there's something cute about this whole mess that leaves me amused more than anything.

Unsure of what to say, I pull her against my chest and kiss the top of her head. I'm about to tell her we need to leave, when someone shines a light over us.

"What's going on back here?"

"Nothing," I growl at the rent-a-cop in the tight yellow T-shirt who's spending too long running his gaze over Athena for my taste.

"Miss, you okay?"

Athena burrows her head against my chest harder. "I'm fine," she yells, but it's mostly muffled by my body.

"I'm gonna need both of you to come out here."

"Fuck off."

Rent-a-cop thinks he's tough. Cracks his knuckles while he lumbers over. Instinctively, I push Athena behind me. Looks like his muscles come from hours at the gym staring at himself in a mirror instead of actual work. I'm going to enjoy kicking the shit out of him.

"You sure about this, boy?" I challenge. It's the only warning he's gonna get.

He stops and shines his light over me again.

"Just checking on the girl," he says while backing up a few steps. *That's right motherfucker, keep going.* "You can't be back here, though."

"We're leaving."

I grab Athena's hand and walk right past the security guard. He backs down fast, because as I suspected, he's a pussy.

"Oh my God. Do you think he saw anything? That was so embarrassing." Athena's high-pitched babble makes me chuckle. Her whole one-minute-she's-on-her-knees-sucking-me-off-and-next-she's-embarrassed attitude is fuckin' cute.

Another band's setting up their gear as we drop back down onto our blanket.

"Have fun, kids?" Dante asks with a dickish grin.

Karina jumps up and grabs Athena's hand. "We're going to grab sodas. Do you want anything?"

Dante hands her some cash and points out which concession stand he wants her to go to—the one he can see from where we are. While Athena rolls her eyes, Karina leans over and kisses the bossy bastard.

He watches them walk all the way up the hill until they're standing in line, then slides his jerkface on and aims it at me.

"So, you ready to pass that bitch around yet?"

My hands fist and he smirks at me knowingly. "Ain't so funny now, is it?" he asks in a low, calm voice meant to remind me of all the shit I've given him since he hooked up with Karina.

"Fuck off. Only reason I'm not knocking your head off your fucking shoulders—"

"Is 'cause you had that coming?" he asks as he stands and waves his hands at me in a *come at me, bro* gesture.

I rise and face him. I don't think my enforcer seriously wants to take a swing at me here in public. Dante's too level-headed to draw that kind of attention our way for no reason. No, he wants to make his point, and because I *have* been a dick to him about his girl, I'll let him. Up until he actually throws a punch. Then it's game on.

"Yes," I admit. That's as much of an apology as he's getting out of me.

He nods and a slow smirk slides over his face. "Thought so." His smirk turns from amused to deadly as he glances the girls' way again.

"Can't let them out of our sight for a second," he grumbles as he takes off up the hill. As soon as I see what's got him so pissed, I'm right behind him.

Athena

I need a drink.

Something fizzy.

Karina elbows me as we walk back up the hill to the concession stands. I try to sneak a glance around us to make sure that security guard isn't in the area.

As if my botched blow job hadn't been bad enough. Almost getting caught by that security guard had been mortifying. Didn't seem to faze Romeo, though.

"What were you doing?" Karina asks while wiggling her eyebrows and laughing at me.

"Nothing you haven't done a hundred times, I'm sure."

Not at all insulted, she laughs even harder and gives me a quick shove.

The line for drinks stretches into the crowd, and we get jostled around while we wait. "Are you sticking around?" she asks without looking at me.

"Well, for another day at least."

Her mouth turns down.

"You said yourself, Kadence won't be back for a few weeks. I'll come home then, promise."

She shakes her head. "It's not that. Romeo seems to like you a lot. Have you told him you're leaving?"

"No." She's going to have a field day with this. "I don't think were at the planning-out-our-lives together stage of our relationship yet."

As I expected, she doubles over laughing, bumping into someone in the crowd.

"Oh, shit, sorry."

She glances up into a familiar face. "Hunter?"

"Hey, Karina." My next-door neighbor lifts his chin at me. "What're you doing here, Athena?"

"We come every year."

"No, I mean your parents have been freaking out."

"What? Why? They know I'm with Karina."

"Well, I guess they tried to stop by her house and found out she doesn't live there anymore." The suspicious glance he casts at Karina makes me want to punch him in the junk.

Karina always thought Hunter was an epic douche, so she doesn't care what he thinks of her. "I moved in with my boyfriend months ago," she says in a bored tone.

I yank my cell phone out of my pocket. Dead. Oops. Guess I was so busy getting laid, I didn't think to charge it. That really says something for Romeo's skills. I'm on my phone so damn much Karina's threatened to jam it in my ass more than once.

"You can use my phone," Hunter offers.

The thought of calling my parents and getting reamed out isn't very appealing. I don't have a chance to answer because two terrifying, pissed off bikers join us. Dante slips an arm around Karina's waist, clearly showing the world who she belongs to. For a second, I have a pang of regret or jealousy or some other stupid emotion. But when Romeo slings his arm around my shoulders in a possessive way, I'm embarrassed to admit to myself, I really like it.

"We were getting worried about you girls," Romeo says. Total lie. More likely they saw us talking to Hunter and decided to check out the situation.

I sort of like the over-protective thing and hate it at the same time. I get enough hovering from my parents. I don't need a man to take over their job.

Suddenly it seems important I continue with my plans to leave for California.

"We're fine," I answer.

Hunter clearly has no idea what to make of Dante and Romeo. Shit. I can only imagine the story he'll run home and tell his parents and then they'll tell my parents and before you know it, the sheriff will be showing up at the Iron Bulls' front door.

Fanfuckingtastic.

Romeo won't want me around if I end up causing him trouble.

That's fine. We all knew how this would end anyway. Maybe I'll get to see him again when I visit Karina.

I try to shift out from underneath his arm, but he tightens his hold on me.

"Who's your friend, sweetheart?" Romeo asks me.

"Uh, Reed, this my next-door neighbor, Hunter. Hunter, this is my, uh...friend, Reed."

I don't miss the disgust that flashes over Hunter's face or the way Dante raises an eyebrow when I use Romeo's real name.

No one fakes politeness and offers to shake a hand.

"Well, okay, then. Good to see you're okay, Athena."

Hunter all but runs away from us.

The guys wait in silence with us while we finally grab our sodas. Karina and Dante go back to our blankets, but Romeo pulls me aside. "What was that about?"

I don't know why I bother playing dumb. "What?"

"That guy. He a boyfriend of yours?"

"No," I answer a little too fast. I'm not used to having such intense interest from a guy.

I can't decide if it's flattering, or really fucking annoying.

SIX

ROMEO

ATHENA'S a big problem for me.

One look at that horny bastard making eyes at my girl had me ready to rip him limb from limb. I prefer to reserve my violent streak for MC business. I don't do jealous boyfriend bullshit. There's no point. Either a bitch wants to fuck me or she doesn't. If one leaves, another one takes her place. That's how it's been since the day I put on my Iron Bulls cut. Only got better once I sewed that President patch on.

This intense, primal need to *stake my claim* on her feels strange, but right.

The way she's quick to say no tells me there's more to the story.

"So he ain't your boyfriend now? Or he's never been a boyfriend?"

She plants her hands on her hips and cocks her head. "Why are you so nosy? I didn't ask you which one of the many half-naked women trolling around your clubhouse you've boinked."

I'm speechless for a second. Not used to backchat from a bitch, but I like it. "We ain't talkin' about me. And you can ask me anything you want, just be prepared for the answers."

"I could tell you the same thing, you know."

Christ, the fuckin' mouth on her gets me hard. I keep staring her down until she huffs and rolls her eyes. I like that she's not easily intimidated. That's an important quality in an ol' lady.

Not that I'm thinking about that.

She takes a deep breath and uses a false-patient voice. "He was never a boyfriend. We fooled around and stuff when we were younger though. Happy now?"

No. Actually, I want to go plant my fists in the kid's face a couple times. A frustrated growl rips out of me, and the little bitch laughs.

"Are you planning to club me over the head and drag me off by my hair now?" she asks.

"Yeah, maybe."

She laughs, as if I won't have the balls to do it, and spins around to head back to our blanket. I catch up quick, grabbing her hand and yanking her against me. "Not so fast, Shortcake."

"What now?"

"How bad you wanna see the rest of the show?"

Her eyes meet mine and her breathing picks up, making her tits rise and fall.

"Why?" she asks, so low I read the question on her lips.

I lean over, bringing my fingers up to wrap them around her neck when I do, and pull her close to whisper in her ear, "Because I want to take you home and bury my tongue in your cunt."

My filthy words make her shiver. I flick my gaze down and find her nipples pressing against the thin cotton of her tank top. "Yeah, I think you'd like that, wouldn't you?"

She can't seem to form any words, but she nods.

We stop by long enough to let Dante know we're leaving. Luck, Amy, and the others have returned, so I don't feel too bad about ditching them. Not that Dante gives a fuck.

Athena can't keep up with me, I'm moving so fast to the exit. People are everywhere, blocking our escape and I fight the urge to smash through the crowd. I make a quick detour to one of those "safer sex" tents with the bowls of condoms and grab a handful, just in case we can't make it back to the clubhouse. Athena laughs.

"Do I want to know?"

"Don't worry about it."

I crouch down in front of her. "Climb on."

"Romeo, you can't carry me out of here."

"Sweetheart, I could bench press you all day long. A piggyback ain't nothing. Now get on."

She wraps her arms around my neck and I hoist her up. Much better. We move through the crowd a whole lot faster this way. She giggles and squeals and chokes the fuck out of me the whole way back to my bike.

When I set her down, she bounces around and lets out a happy squeal. "That was fun."

Her happiness turns my mouth up, and I'm usually a pretty cranky son of a bitch. But her enthusiasm is contagious. I like how she makes me feel.

When we're finally on the road, she starts gettin' frisky. At first I think it's an accident that she brushes her hand over my crotch. But pretty soon she's steadily rubbing my dick through my jeans.

She keeps it up we're gonna crash.

I pull off the highway into a wooded area and shut the bike down.

"What? Where are we?" Athena asks.

"Get off," I growl.

She dismounts and stands next to me with wide eyes. I get a sick thrill watching her tremble with uncertainty while I stare her down. "You're a bad girl. That's dangerous, messin' with the driver."

Her bottom lip pushes out into the sexiest fuckin' pout. "I couldn't help myself," she says in a low sex-kitten voice. I sit back and yank her over my lap to paddle her ass a few times. She yipes, kicks, and giggles. Then she's gasping as I work my hands under her, undo her jeans and yank them down over her hips. My bare hand on her bare ass feels a whole lot better.

For me anyway.

This time she shrieks.

"Ow! You fucker. Cut it out."

I push a finger in her pussy and find her soaking wet. "Don't lie, Athena. Your body says you like it."

"Bullshit. I'm worked up from before."

"Liar."

We're off the road, but not exactly hidden. I doubt anyone can see what we're doing, but the sounds of cars rushing by and the occasional lights wash over us, reminding me we're not alone. Getting caught would probably be unpleasant. Might end up with a ticket. Might end up in jail for the night.

It still doesn't stop me from helping her sit up and face me, back to the handlebars. "Lift up."

She does as I ask for once, and I yank her pants off, taking her sneakers with them. "Hey!"

"Shut up."

She helps me work my jeans open and free my dick. Thankful for the condoms I grabbed, I take one out and get it on pretty fuckin' fast. I pat my thighs. "Put your feet here."

Takes her a second to figure it out, but finally, she's sinking down on my cock and I groan so loud, I probably scare every coyote and jackrabbit within five miles away.

"Fuck me, I never should have let you out of my bed today."

She moans in agreement and grabs my shoulders so she can work herself up and down my dick.

"Good girl."

"Are you sure we won't tip over?"

"I got us, sweetheart. You just worry about riding my dick."

"I—I—am," she stammers out in a breathless whisper. "I can't."

"Lean back."

She does as I ask, thrusting her breasts up and I slide her shirt up so I can see them better. "Thank fuck you're flexible," I mumble while keeping one hand on her hip.

"Romeo, I'm...I'm—"

"Good. Give it."

She sobs and moans and shakes apart as she comes.

Feels so fucking good, it triggers me. I give her a second to breathe before pulling her off me and helping her dress.

When we're cleaned up I curl an arm around her, bringing her close for a kiss. "That will hold me until we get back to the clubhouse."

"Oh my God." She laughs and leans up to kiss my cheek. "You're crazy."

If I'm crazy it's all because of her. I'm known for being cold, calculating, and level-headed. Not with her, though.

She's a big risk in my life.

Athena

We make it back to the clubhouse with no more stops. Well, unless you count Romeo pushing me up against the clubhouse wall and kissing me until my heart pounds. We're interrupted by two guys who barely look old enough to drive, let alone be members. Romeo growls an unhappy greeting at them.

"Wolf's looking for ya," one says.

"Where's he at?"

"Chapel."

"You have a chapel here?" I ask when Romeo pulls me inside.

"Not that kind of chapel, honey," he answers.

His eyes are already searching the clubhouse, so I assume he has things he needs to take care of. "I feel all sweaty and dirty. Do you mind if I go up and take a shower?"

"Not at all." Digging into his pocket, he pulls out a set

of keys, slips one off and hands it to me. "Lock the door behind you. I have another key."

"Okay."

He tucks me up tight against his body and leans down to whisper in my ear. "Get yourself clean, so I can get you filthy again."

His lips move from my ear, along my jaw, and finally press against my mouth before he releases me.

It takes a second to find my feet and start moving toward the stairs.

Romeo's room is in sight when one of the doors on my left opens and Melody steps out. She's busy fixing her top and doesn't see me right away, but it's impossible to move past her without her noticing me.

"Shocked *you're* still here. You're not really his type."

If she thinks I'm surprised or insulted, I'm about to disappoint her. "I know. Weird, right?" I answer in a voice laced with sarcasm that probably goes right over her empty head. I don't stop for her reaction, but she lobs another verbal bullet my way before I work Romeo's door open.

"You know he's just using you to get close to Karina, right?"

"Good to know." I raise my hand and wave without turning around and shut the door firmly behind me.

That's stupid, right? I mean, Karina's so obviously with Dante. And from the little I've seen, these guys don't fuck around with another brother's woman.

Then again, Karina's hinted in a thousand—not so subtle—ways how much she dislikes Romeo.

Maybe there's more to the story.

SEVEN

ROMEO

"WHAT?" I ask as soon as I step in the chapel. Yeah, club comes first. But right now, there's a hot naked woman in my shower that I'd rather be dealing with, than anything my VP's gotta tell me.

"Tucker's a problem."

"No shit."

"I'm serious. He made a detour. Went right through Red Storm territory, and I'm pretty sure he had a sit-down with Deacon."

Well, fuck me. Karina's father really must have a death wish.

Wolf all but snaps his fingers in my face when I don't answer him right away. "How do you want to handle it?"

"My plan was to let him get through these next few shipments, then hand him over to Dante to deal with." Dante's got lots of reasons to want Tucker dead. But now that it looks like Tucker's trying to get protection from one of our rivals, it might be time to move up his execution date.

Wolf's eyebrows draw down. He doesn't know the full story about why Dante's got it out for Karina's father. And it ain't my business to tell it. From what I know, after the way Tucker's treated both his daughters, he's earned every bit of pain coming his way.

"How do you wanna play it?"

"Let's see how he acts when he comes in." I didn't land in this chair by making rash decisions. Although, every day that I'm forced to tolerate Tucker's fuck-ups, I'm rethinking my decision not to kill him back when I found him rippin' me off.

Wolf opens his mouth to argue with me, and I hold up a hand. "It ain't for discussion, brother." I ain't touching a tire inside Red Storm territory without good reason. And Tucker ain't a good reason to risk myself or my men.

"Our alliance with Bolt's crew is solid."

"Solid *now*." After way too many concessions in my opinion. "Savage Dragons got beef with Tucker, too. I ain't wasting any favors on him."

"What if he don't come back?"

"Then we're out a couple grand. Tucker don't know shit that could hurt us."

"Okay, Prez."

Finally. Fuck me, but I get tired of explaining every fuckin' move I make sometimes.

Thank fuck no one else is waiting to stop me from getting back to Athena when I leave the chapel. Well, none of my brothers.

Melody stops me in the hallway.

"You need something new tonight?"

"Nope. I'm good, honey."

"Maybe a third?"

"No," I answer without even considering the offer. Since up until last night Athena was a virgin, I don't think me bringing in another girl will make her too happy. I don't stop to examine my lack of interest or how much I need Athena all to myself.

When I step into my room, the running water from the bathroom gets my dick hard. My feisty lil' bitch is in there.

My clothes hit the floor so fast it isn't even funny.

The outline of her slick body is visible through the glass, working me up even more. The sounds of her singing softly stop me.

Shit, that's cute.

She lets out a little scream when I open the door. I play big, bad protector and wrap her up in my arms, getting soaked in the process. "It's just me."

Her little hand whacks my chest. "You scared the shit out of me."

"Sorry."

"Everything okay?"

"Yeah. It will be."

She peers up at me. "President of a motorcycle club is more than just riding hogs and clubhouse orgies, isn't it?"

I snort at the question. "Yeah, Shortcake."

"Do you do bad things?"

"Sometimes."

"Should I be scared?"

"No. You're safe with me."

She rests her cheek against my chest and I squeeze her a little tighter. Her arms wrap around my middle and we stand there under the spray for a bit. It's nice. Peaceful.

I have few peaceful moments in my life. I'm not complaining. It's just a fact. So this one, I'm enjoying the fuck out of.

After a few minutes, peaceful turns to playful. Athena's hands slide down over my ass and she gropes me.

"You have a nice tushy," she murmurs.

Honest to God, it's the funniest compliment a woman has ever given me, and I burst out laughing.

Her girlish giggles fill the shower stall. "Stop making fun of me."

"I'm not. You're cute." She makes a few good-natured grumbly noises. "Hey, I never asked. What're you doing this summer?"

Her gaze slips away from mine and she lifts her shoulders. "Not much."

"You doing that hospital internship with Karina?"

She glances up at me in surprise. "Why do you know what Karina's doing?"

Why is that weird? Dante's girl's in my clubhouse all the time. Plus, he never shuts the fuck up about her. "I don't know. Dante's mentioned it a bunch of times."

"Oh."

Her hands slide over my ass again, her little nails raking into skin. "Careful, Shortcake."

This time she's feeling flirty. She bats her long, wet lashes a few times. "Why? Are you going to spank me again?"

Using my bigger body, I shove her up against the slick tile wall, caging her in with my forearms. Her doe in the headlights eyes stare up at me with so much innocence, I almost want her to close them, so she doesn't see all the filthy ways I want to use her body. One of my big hands slides into her hair, cupping the back of her head so I can lower my mouth to hers. Pushing my tongue past her parted lips to taste her. She moans into my mouth and rises on her toes, then slips, grabbing my shoulders to keep her balance.

"Careful," I whisper, as I pull back.

My cock's like steel against her soft belly, and her hands stroke down my arms, over my hips, finally wrapping around me. "Can I try again?"

She's too sweet for a man like me.

I nod anyway, because the way she keeps staring at my dick and licking her lips? No, isn't an option.

Athena

Excitement and fear clash inside me. My hands continue to lazily slide up and down Romeo's impressive cock. Well, impressive to me. I don't exactly have a lot to compare it to. It feels amazing and he knows how to use it. That's all that matters.

"You won't come in my mouth again?" I ask.

Romeo's lips quirk but he rubs the back of his hand over my cheek. "No, sweetheart."

He could repeat the alphabet in that low, rumbly voice, and I'd be ready to drop to my knees.

This time I want to make it good. Show him I'm not a stupid little girl. My hands continue to stroke up and down his shaft. At least there's enough light to admire him fully. I take my time kissing my way down his chest, which he seems to appreciate. His groans of satisfaction vibrate through me, arousal right behind it.

Balancing myself by gripping his legs, I lower myself to the shower floor. The water turns cool and Romeo shifts to adjust the temperature.

I stare at his cock for so long, he chuckles. "Lick me."

His hand threads into my hair, brushing wet strands from my forehead and I lean forward to take a taste. Above me, he hisses, and I raise my eyes to find him staring down at me.

"Good girl," he whispers hoarsely. "Now, open wider."

A little fear runs through me as he positions himself to thrust into my mouth. He's *big*. But he takes his time, slowly sliding his cock into my mouth. The salty taste of him doesn't bother me this time, and I close my mouth around him. My hands work up and down as he moves faster, fucking my mouth deeper with each thrust until I choke. He pulls back and our eyes meet again.

"Okay?" he asks.

I nod and open my mouth wider, sticking my tongue out in a completely obscene way that I'd never do with someone else. But I feel free to explore and do anything that comes over me with him. Especially when he growls and thrusts back into my mouth. "Pretty girl, take it all for me," he grunts out. Our eyes lock as he watches for any sign I'm not loving this, and it makes me feel safe enough to relax.

"Touch yourself," he demands. "Pinch your nipples for me."

As if he holds a remote control to my body, my hands leave him to cup my breasts, squeezing.

"Harder."

The second my fingers close over the tight peaks, I moan and he curses, pulling out and shooting cum all over my chest.

"Jesus. Fucking hell. Fuck." He's breathing hard, braced against the wall, but after a second, he glances down and offers me a hand. He pulls me off the floor into his arms and takes my mouth in a deep kiss.

"Was that better?" I ask when we part.

His mouth turns up. "Fuck yeah."

He turns me toward the spray, cleaning me off. When he's finished, his lips brush against my ear. "I need you in my bed."

"Okay." He seems different as he slaps the faucet off and grabs a towel. He dries me carefully. Kneeling puts him at eye level with my breasts and he stares at them for a few seconds. As I'm about to ask what he's doing, he cups them, flicking his thumbs over the pebbled tips.

"Oh," I whisper, then gasp as he sucks one into his mouth, pulling away slowly until my nipple is trapped between his teeth. My hands dig into his hair, holding him to me, but giving him enough room to suck and nibble at my other breast.

"Reed, fuck." My hushed voice sounds ten times louder against his heavy breathing in the tiny bathroom.

"In a minute."

I'm too frenzied to laugh. He stands and picks me up, sealing his mouth against mine and carrying us to the bedroom. I bounce a little when he tosses me on the mattress, but he follows, pushing me backward and parting my legs. It freaks me out to have him study my private area so my legs close. Or they would if he hadn't wedged his arms between them.

"Why are you staring at me?"

For a brief second, he flicks his gaze up and meets my eyes. "Because you're fucking beautiful."

Heat sears my skin at his simple, honest statement. "Oh." He's so completely comfortable naked, staring at my pussy like it's no big deal. And I realize that's because for him it's *not* a big deal. He's probably done this hundreds of times.

"What's wrong?" he asks as he lays down, tossing my legs over his shoulders and running his hands over my thighs.

"Nothing. No one's ever paid such close attention to *down there*."

He grunts and uses his thumbs to spread my lips. "Men eat pussy, Athena. Don't waste your time on ones who don't."

My stomach clenches at the reminder. Whatever we're doing here is only short-term. I know that. But I can't be upset about it. *I'm* the one leaving for L.A. soon.

I don't have a chance to respond, because he closes his mouth over my clit. My hips shoot up, grinding into his face, because that is ah-ma-*zing*. *Holy fucksticks!*

His groans of approval are muffled because I keep

pushing harder into his face. His hands slide under my butt, pulling me closer, holding me up so he can *feast*. It's the only way to describe what he's doing.

"Holy fuckcakes!"

He chuckles and keeps right on licking me into oblivion. He pushes one finger in me, and pumps it steadily until I'm whimpering and so close to the edge I want to explode.

When he adds a second finger, I'm done. "Reed!"

He makes this "Uh-hmm" sound but doesn't take his mouth off me for a second.

After what seems like an eternity of bliss, I'm limp. Reed pulls away, grinning and wiping his face. "You're so fucking sweet. Could do that all night."

I'm still sensitive and tingly everywhere so I sort of grunt in response, which makes him laugh. My head rolls to the side to watch him while he rubs his thick cock. "Need to fuck you now. You up for it?"

"I think so."

He gestures to his nightstand. "Grab me a condom."

I turn but can't quite reach.

"Hurry, or I'll come on your pretty little tits."

Finally, I snag one and toss it to him. He's severely sexy as he rips into the package and slides the rubber on. His hands grip my thighs, spreading me wide, but his eyes are watching me as he nudges his cock in slow. "Your wet little cunt is perfect."

No one's ever said such crude things to me before. But I love it.

It feels wrong, but in all the best ways.

Romeo

I can't get enough of this girl.

She drained me dry in the shower, but a few minutes with my face buried in her cunt and I'm ready to go again. Our eyes lock. She flinches a little when I push all the way inside. Slow and steady, without stopping. I pull back and she lifts up, asking for more.

"You like that?"

"Fuck. Yes."

"You've got a filthy mouth on you when you're getting fucked."

She grins and holds her hands out to me. How can I say no to a little cuddlefucking? I fall down over her, careful not to crush her and gather her up while I continue pumping slow and deep.

"I want to see you come."

She whines and moans. Her body trembles and her chest flushes a deep red. I want to take one of her nipples between my lips again, but I wasn't kidding about wanting to see her come. I want to watch her let go. As soon as I move faster, and harder, she goes over and I go right with her.

For some reason I can't stop kissing her, but she kisses me back just as fierce. Our foreheads touch and I stare straight into her eyes.

Something warm shifts in my chest and I pull back. Shake it off.

"Reed?"

Her soft hands run up and down my back, distracting me. "Baby, I gotta toss this."

She reaches up and gives me one more kiss, then releases me.

When I stumble back from the bathroom, she's dressed in the same club T-Shirt I gave her to sleep in last night.

"Want you naked tonight."

Her lips curl into a smirk and she twists her hands into the hem of the shirt, slowly sliding it up and off.

"Don't fuck with me, Shortcake."

"I'm not."

"Yeah, you are. Get in bed."

"I need to use the bathroom."

Waiting for her is torture, even though she's probably not even gone five minutes. When she finally emerges, she's busy twisting her hair into two long braids.

"What's with the pigtails? You trying to make me feel like a pervy old man?"

She giggles and jumps onto the mattress next to me. "No. My hair's still wet. I always braid it if I go to sleep with wet hair."

I reach out to grab one of the ends, flicking it over her nipple. "Cute."

She pins me with a serious look, and I know whatever's pinging in her head means trouble. "How old *are* you?"

"Too old for you."

Her mouth turns down and she moves away. My hand shoots out, wrapping around her ankle. "I didn't mean—"

"No. I get it. Maybe I should—"

"Don't." I sit up and throw the covers back. "Get in here."

Reluctantly, she slides into bed and settles next to me.

"I like you, Athena."

"Why? You don't know anything about me."

"I know you have a smart mouth and don't have a problem saying what's on your mind."

She snorts and turns away. "I thought all you big, badass bikers like their women to keep quiet."

I think about how to answer her. While that's true to some extent, as president, I also need a ballsy bitch who doesn't take shit from anyone. Not to mention that smart mouth of hers gets me harder than a motherfucker. "Out there, don't ever sass me. In here, run your mouth all you want. I'll stick my dick in it when I need you to be quiet."

"You're a pig."

"Yeah." What's the point of disagreeing?

With the lights off, I can barely make out the curve of her shoulder. I reach out and trace my fingers over it and down her arm.

"Where do your parents think you are?"

"Camping with Karina." She turns and faces me. "They'd kill me if they knew I was here."

"I got that impression at your graduation."

"I'm a big girl." The way she says it sounds more like she's trying to convince herself.

I want to say "no you're not. You're too innocent to realize what a mistake you're making with me." But I keep my mouth shut.

Even if it's wrong, I want her to stay.

EIGHT

ATHENA

I WAKE with Romeo staring at me again.

"You know, it's really creepy to watch people in their sleep."

He laughs so hard, my head bounces around on his chest. "Don't be so pretty then."

His fingers tickle over my side, making me laugh, too.

Finally, he settles down and takes my chin in his hand, turning me to face him. "Since you let me violate you all weekend, I should ask if you got any special requests."

"Special requests?"

"Yeah. Anything you want to try?" He taps the side of my head. "What do you think about?"

I sit up and stare at him, admiring all his muscle and beautiful ink. "What do you mean?"

"Like, I've pictured you on your knees with my cock down your throat ten times a day since we met. We did that yesterday and we'll do it again soon."

"Oh." His words paint a vivid picture of all the things we've done and a wave of arousal washes over me.

Suddenly, I know *exactly* what I want. I just don't know how to say it without him thinking I'm a weirdo.

"Athena?"

I try to look away, but he grabs my chin again, forcing me to look at him. "Tell me."

"Video? I've always wondered what it'd be like—"

A feral grin turns his mouth up. "Ah. My girl's got a bit of porn star in her. Nice."

There's a whole bunch in that sentence I don't know what to do with. Starting with him calling me *his girl*. "Hmm…if I'm a porn star, it's because you make me feel like one. Remember, a few days ago I was just an innocent little virgin?" I whisper the last part against his lips.

"There's nothing innocent about what you do to my dick, Shortcake." His rich, low laughter lights a fire in my belly and I wriggle against him. My hand brushes over his cock. He wasn't lying, he's thick and hard. Ready for me.

"Is that for me?" I tease.

"No one else."

The heat under my skin burns hotter. It's not only his words. It's his scent. The way he stares at me. The way his fingers expertly roll my nipples, squeezing and tugging just the right amount. He leans down and captures one in his mouth, sucking hard. His stubbly chin scrapes against me, while one hand continues pulling at my other nipple.

My fingers twine into his hair, holding him against me. He growls, releases my nipple and attacks the other one.

Forgetting what we'd been talking about. What led to this, I arch my back and surrender to whatever he wants to do to me.

Then he stops. He sits up, taking me with him. "Let's save it for the camera. I've got one around here somewhere."

It takes a second for the words to fall into place and make sense in my lust-soaked head. "Whoa, wait. We're doing it now?"

"Oh, fuck yeah."

"Can I go to the bathroom first?"

"Go ahead. I'll get it set up."

Nervous and excited, I swipe my bag off the floor on the way to the bathroom and lock myself inside.

Am I really doing this?

Fantasizing about playing porn star is completely different from actually doing it. But I don't want to talk myself out of it. Instead, I tear through my bag, which happens to be filled with a bunch of sexy stuff I haven't even worn yet, since Romeo's pretty much demanded I'm naked when we're in his room.

What had seemed so sexy in the middle of Victoria's Secret the other day, now seems tame compared to what I've seen most of the girls running around this clubhouse in. But it's the best I've got and I still think it's pretty.

I slip the pink and black baby-doll nightie over my head and tie the long satin ties behind my neck. The front parts into two floaty pieces and I smooth them over my hips before sliding the tiny panties up and tying them at the sides.

Am I nuts? Nothing seems hotter than being watched while being sexy. While having sex. Capturing those fleeting moments and watching them together later must be the ultimate turn-on.

Before I chicken out, I fling open the door. My jaw drops.

Romeo's sitting on the bed fiddling with a small camera. While I was changing, he dimmed the lights to a seductive level, smoothed out the sheets, and lit a candle. How does such a hard, brutal man even own a candle?

He glances up and freezes. For a second, I don't even think he takes a breath. His dark blue eyes are full of such intensity, I'm speechless.

"Ready?" he asks. As if the panty-wetting decor isn't enough, his low, sexy voice heats all my bare skin.

I'm barely breathing as I nod and strike what I hope is a sexy pose in the doorway. He lifts the camera and a little red light blinks steadily.

"Tell me what we're doing, Shortcake."

My hand moves to play with the ribbon between my breasts. It's a nervous gesture, but must look sexy to Romeo because he sucks in a deep breath.

"Shit, you're fucking hot." He lifts his chin. "Tell me."

"You're going to film us."

"Doing what? Be specific."

"While we fuck."

"Yeah? What else?"

I'm not sure what to say.

"You gonna ride my dick for the camera?"

"Oh, yes."

"Gonna come for me on camera?"

"Yes."

"Get over here."

I run my hands over the material of the baby-doll and his response is barely human. With a throaty growl, he sets the camera on his dresser—at the right height to catch everything that happens on his bed—and mauls me. His hands grip my ass, yanking me to him while his mouth closes over mine. All power and want. For me.

I'm breathing hard when we part and I have to ask one last question.

"Promise me you won't show it to anyone else."

He stares down at me and brushes the back of his hand over my cheek. "No problem there, Shortcake. No one else sees my girl naked."

There it is again. *My girl.*

I hate how much I like it.

Romeo

If I owned anything resembling a conscience, I wouldn't do this. But when a hot girl you're fucking says she'd like to fuck in front of a camera, you get the fucking camera out.

It's not like I want to exploit her and load it onto some website to make a quick buck. I wasn't kidding about no one seeing our video. She's mine. I ain't lettin' anyone see what belongs to me.

She's a crazy contradiction of innocence and naughty girl, standing there in a whispy, see-through, pink and black lace nightie. I pick up the camera again, aiming it at her while I back away and drop down on the bed.

"Show me."

Everything she's feeling flickers over her eyes and face. The way she swings from sexy confidence to nervous innocence. She wants this, but she's scared. The sick fucker inside me who feeds on her fear, loves it.

Confidence seems to win over and she makes a show of fluffing her breasts, playing peek-a-boo with the thin, floating material and flicking the ties at her hips. Her pretty pink-tipped tits are visible through barely-there fabric. I can't wait to rip every piece of lace right off her.

She smiles as if she's letting me in on a secret and unties the bow between her breasts, flashing me. Just a tease. I'm loving this and hating it at the same time.

"Now, you show me," she says in a voice barely above a whisper.

While trying to be bossy is cute on her, I'm not ready for this to end yet. "You haven't earned it yet, Shortcake. Take your top off nice and slow."

She stretches her arms over her head, untying it and letting it float to the floor.

I reward her with an encouraging, "Very pretty." Then aim the camera at her tits. "Touch yourself."

She seems to know exactly what I want, cupping her tits, and teasing her nipples for me. Her laughter's low and dirty as she slides a hand down over her belly and under the front of her panties.

"I didn't say you could touch your pussy."

"You didn't say I couldn't, either," she sasses back. That fucking mouth of hers is hot as hell.

"Get that sexy ass over here." She turns and gives me a peek at her ass before taking slow, deliberate steps my way. I'm so fucking hard, my dick's poking out of my briefs waving hello.

"On your knees," I say when she reaches me. She leans

over, pushing her tits in my face, placing her hands on my legs to lower herself to the floor with the ease of a cat.

She flicks her fearless blue eyes up and slicks her tongue across her bottom lip, slow for the camera.

"You're gorgeous." It's too bad I have no shame. The filthy, depraved things I want to do to this girl ain't right —but this is her game and there's no way I'm passing on it.

"Tell me what you want, Romeo," she says, using her sex-kitten voice.

I hold back a chuckle. Who the hell am I around this girl? Someone without the weight of running an MC around my neck for sure. Someone who laughs.

"Take my dick out."

She gets to work while I train the camera on her hands, diving inside my briefs. Fuck it. I lift up so she can work them down my legs and toss 'em.

"Wrap your hand around me."

Warm fingers stroke up and down my cock and her head tips down. "Do you want my mouth on you?" she asks.

She doesn't wait for an answer. No, she swirls her tongue around the head of my cock, unhinging my brain. I settle one hand on her back and keep the camera on her with the other. I keep my touch light, afraid I'll lose it and hurt her. Force her head down until her nose hits my crotch.

Done teasing, she lowers her head and swallows my dick in one deep suck. *Fuck.* Her lips around me, the hollowing of her cheeks as she sucks, I get it all on film before the wet searing heat races to my head and I have to set the camera down.

After bobbing and teasing for a while, she glances up, staring into my eyes.

"Suck like a good little porn star."

She chuckles, the vibrations adding to my pleasure. She should be terrified. Every pull of her mouth makes me lose a little more control. I can't last like this.

Grabbing her hair, I pull her off me with a soft popping noise.

"Get up in the bed."

She grins and scrambles up behind me. I take a second to pose her the way I want for the camera and kneel between her legs.

This time when our eyes meet, I think she sees the dark violence brewing inside me. She shivers, and her smile fades.

"Spread your legs."

She's quick to do it. Even brings her hands down and spreads her lips.

"Good girl," I breathe out. Starting nice and slow, I lick from her opening to her clit. I stop and graze my teeth over her sensitive flesh and she gasps.

"Like that?"

"Yes," she whispers. One of her hands threads into my hair, nails raking against my scalp.

"That's good. Show me what you like, Athena."

I lick her again, but she's still tense. "Relax and breathe. Forget the camera."

She nods and I watch her take a few deep breaths before getting back to business. The sucking rhythm of my lips and tongue against her clit makes her cry out. Hard breathing, little high-pitched noises. So many beautiful fucking sounds she makes. The prettiest sound of all is when I thrust a finger in her snug little cunt, and she yells out my name.

"Reed! Please."

I add another finger and keep fucking her, licking her.

"Oh, oh, oh." She shakes under me.

"Come, sweetheart. All over my face. Don't hold back."

She just makes a series of noises in response, and I laugh against her clit. "Got no words?"

She alternates between "Yes, no, and please." Over and over again until she can't hold back. Her hips buck off the bed, and I keep right on pulsing my fingers in and out until I'm drowning in her juices.

"Good girl," I keep encouraging, while she shudders and moans through her orgasm.

She holds her arms out and I crawl up her body, stopping to kiss and lick her along the way. Finally, I get to her neck where I nuzzle, lick, and inhale her girly scent. We're nowhere near finished, but I give her a few seconds before reaching out, grabbing a condom and rolling it on.

My eyes close as I stop to kiss her. Not for the camera. For me, for her, because I love kissing her soft lips. She arches up as I slide into her. Wet, tight heat clenches around my dick. Tingles race up my spine and over my skin.

"Reed," she whispers. Breathless. Gasping as I rock into her faster. "Don't stop."

"No. Can't." My hands grip her waist, holding her, staking a claim. "You're mine. My girl."

She moans but doesn't answer.

I reach between us and drag my thumb over her clit, and she yelps. "My pussy, Athena. Mine. Say it."

"Yours. I'm all yours. Only yours."

"Better." Fuck, it's so good my brain's about to crack in two. "You need to come for me, sweetheart."

"I'm trying."

"Don't try." I close my mouth over one tight nipple, licking and sucking, while I stroke two fingers over her clit in fierce circles. She's gonna come for me or I'll die trying.

A few seconds later, her body wrenches tight, she jerks under me, moans, and digs her nails into my shoulders.

I let go after that. She's so beautiful. Jacking waves of pleasure take hold of me. White hot rushes of satisfaction. Like nothing—and I mean nothing—I've ever felt before. I press kisses against her shoulder and neck, inhale her sex-sweat scented skin and slowly come back to myself.

Shifting my weight off her, I ditch the condom. I use my last bit of energy to push myself up and shut off the camera.

"Tomorrow, we'll watch that. Maybe do it all over again."

She giggles and runs her leg against mine. "I don't know if I can."

I slide back down into the bed and snuggle her under the covers. She curls up against me like she belongs there. And she does.

The sex is fantastic, but I also want to know more

about her. Know *her*. And strangely, I want her to know me.

"I want to take you to my shop tomorrow."

Big, blue eyes blink a few times before she asks, "How come?"

"I'd like you to see where I spend a lot of my time. Maybe show you a few projects I'm working on."

She hesitates before answering. "Okay. Sounds like fun."

I hug her a little tighter and kiss her forehead. The warmth of her snuggling closer eases any doubts about taking this risk.

NINE

ROMEO

I'm rudely interrupted from our post-sex nap by my VP sending me a handful of texts.

Athena's sound asleep on her stomach, her perfect little ass sticking up enough to make it real fuckin' hard to get out of bed without fucking her again.

Hopefully, she'll be like that when I return.

My dick gets hard thinking of watching that video with her later. Thinking of new things I want to film. This could turn into a full-time habit.

What's waiting for me downstairs is the fuck who's been nothing but a pain in my ass for months now.

Tucker. Karina's father.

"What?" I snap as I lead him into my office.

"Can you call Dante down too?"

"Jesus, fuck. Really?" But I'm already yanking my phone out to send him a text.

I give him a pointed look after I set my phone down. "I'm tryin' to make things right. That guy I hired to scare Karina…the one she said…hurt her? I tracked him down." He waves a piece of paper in the air. "Think you can keep Dante from killing me if I hand it over?"

I roll my eyes, because honestly, no. My enforcer isn't some pit bull I keep on a leash. "It's a start."

The big, snarling bastard shows up a few minutes later. "What do you want?" he growls when he sees Tucker. I wave him in and point to the seat farthest from Tucker—just in case.

"Tucker's got some info for you."

Dante shows the barest hint of interest.

"The guy who—"

"Molested your daughter?" I add helpfully. I hate this pansy fuck who never takes any responsibility for his actions.

He acts as if I hadn't spoken, but his cheeks turn red. How such a sweet, gentle, smart girl can be related to this man baffles me. Thank fuck I'm the one who bought his debt and not someone else. This piece of shit would have had her turning tricks on a street corner to support his gambling habit. The irony of her ending up with a severe motherfucker like Dante is pretty funny.

"If she says so. I still don't believe—"

"Shut the fuck up," Dante snaps. "I know it's hard for you to grasp this concept, but Karina doesn't lie to me."

Tucker has some balls. He doesn't react at all. Just continues. "This guy was with Red Storm MC. One of their East Coast charters, but he went nomad. Name's Hardy. He goes by Viper or something stupid like that."

"Yeah. Where's he now?"

"People I talked to think he's either in Texas or Nevada. Deacon's looking for him too."

That's...odd. Also odd that they'd give an outsider any information about a brother. "Why? If he's nomad, what's Deacon's crew care?"

Tucker shrugs. "I think he fucked someone over. Either he's *out bad* or he's marked. I don't really know much more than that."

"Well, at least you're not completely useless for once," Dante says, snatching the paper out of Tucker's hand.

"That's a shit picture. What the fuck am I supposed to do with that?" he asks, then tosses it my way.

"Best I could get," Tucker whines.

I raise an eyebrow at Dante, and he stands. "I'll put Luck on it."

Figures. Luck seems to be the only brother Dante trusts one hundred percent with his girl. Fuck only knows what the three of them are up to. Dante leaves, and Tucker gets up to leave as well.

"Sit back down. We ain't finished."

Guilt flashes over his face. "What do you need?"

"This why you were up in Red Storm territory when you were supposed to be delivering our shit?"

"Yeah. I got a lead and followed it. Your stuff made it there on time." He's not lying. I got confirmation of it last night. Still fucking irritated he took a risk with club assets.

He pulls out an envelope and hands it over. "I even

got some cash to pay my debt, since it looks like you and Karina ain't gonna be a thing. You know I'm real sorry."

I roll my eyes—Karina and I were never going to be a *thing*— but I snatch up the envelope. "Who'd you borrow it from?"

"No one."

Tucker's a shit liar. But I don't give a fuck who he ripped off to pay me back.

"Oh, I also heard about Logan. He might be up in Seattle."

"Think he's trying to cross into Canada?"

"Maybe. What did he do? He's patched, right?"

"Ain't your concern. It's club business."

"Come on. I've known him since he was a kid. If you're gonna kill him, I'd like to know."

"Like I said, it doesn't concern you. It's club business." It's actually Dante's business. Logan kidnapped Karina. Dante's got every right to kill the little traitor. Of course, it's more complicated than that. Then the thought of anyone taking Athena from me burns through my veins. Nope. Not complicated at all.

I'd kill anyone who came between us.

Athena

After eighteen years of gentle treatment, the pounding my pussy's taken the last few days is enough that I'm a little relieved to wake up alone.

I bury my nose in Romeo's pillow. The way I respond to his scorched grass and wind scent makes a liar out of my abused girly-bits. I'd jump him right this second if he was here.

Where is he?

I slip into another one of his club shirts. This one's faded to a dull steel gray and soft. The club's pissed-off bull on the back and "Prez" on the front. I'm guessing there aren't a lot of these. I wonder if he'll mind that I'm wearing it.

If we were at his house, or somewhere with any privacy, I'd just wear the shirt. But I could encounter any number of people in this clubhouse, so I slip on a pair of stretchy pants and head downstairs.

A familiar voice stops me from pushing my way into Romeo's office. Mr. Rivers? Karina's father. How does he even know someone like Romeo?

Then the words he said sink in.

"Looks like you and Karina ain't gonna be a thing. Sorry about that."

Romeo was interested in my best friend? Blood roars through my ears, drowning out anything else.

"You okay, darlin'?"

I'm jolted by a gentle hand on my shoulder and stare up into a stern, but not unkind face. "Luck, right?" I squeak out.

"Yeah. You looking for Romeo?"

"Sort of."

His mouth tips into a smile at my vague answer. "Why don't you wait by the bar?" He reaches past me and shuts the door to Romeo's office.

We don't make it to the bar before Romeo's door opens. I turn, hoping to see him, but it's Karina's dad leaving. "Hi, Mr. Rivers," I call out. Behind me, Luck laughs.

"Athena? What the hell are you doing here?"

"I, uh...came with Karina."

"You shouldn't—"

"She's with *me*." Romeo's big frame fills the doorway and he muscles past Mr. Rivers. "You lookin' for me, Shortcake?" The harsh tone of his voice and expression on his face softens as he approaches me.

"Yeah, kinda."

I think the smile on his face is the first one I've seen outside the bedroom, and it's completely focused on me. I sway a little on my feet, and he wraps me up in his arms, picking me up for a not-so-quick kiss.

When he sets me down, Mr. Rivers is gone.

"How do you know Karina's dad?"

His smile vanishes. "That's club business."

My lips part for a follow up question, but he places a finger over my mouth. "Not your concern."

The hot flare of my temper rising must be visible on my face. Romeo's eyebrow quirks. "You offended, Shortcake?"

"Yes," I snap as I turn to head upstairs.

He wraps his hand around my arm, pulling me back. "That's the way it is around here. Ol' ladies stay out of club business," he says against my neck.

Confused, I shake out of his grasp. "I'm not an old lady."

"No," he agrees, so quietly I have to lean in closer to hear him. "Not yet."

TEN

ATHENA

ALL NIGHT I'm back and forth in my head. Wait to explain to Romeo that I'm headed to California, or make a clean split?

I'm afraid if I tell him my plans, he'll try to make me stay. And I'm afraid I won't be strong enough to say no.

I already sent my deposit to my roommate weeks ago. Signed up for my acting class. I *have* to go.

That whole thing with Karina's father and Romeo maybe being interested in her has been bothering me too. Even with him sound asleep next to me, I can't shake the bad feelings that followed me all day after overhearing that conversation.

It wouldn't be the first time a guy tried to use me to get close to my best friend.

I change my mind a thousand times as I slip out of bed, slide on a pair of jeans, collect my things, and scribble out a quick note.

Luck's downstairs at the bar.

"Hey, Athena."

I strain for a casual attitude. "Hey. You're at the bar early."

"Inventory, darlin'. Not drinking."

"Oh."

"Where you headed?"

"Um, home. Just need to check in with my parents before they like call the National Guard or something."

He chuckles. "Good plan. Will we see you later?"

"Sure."

I'm shaking like a leaf by the time I get into my car.

Why?

We haven't made any promises to each other. He's not my *boyfriend*. I don't have to run my life decisions by him.

Common courtesy, nitwit.

I ignore that little voice.

Romeo

I know I'm alone in my bed before I even open my eyes. No soft, warm girl curled up against me. The knowledge fully pulls me from sleep.

"Athena?"

The room's completely still and quiet. Sitting up, I take notice of the fact that her bag's gone. My eyes dart to every surface her stuff had been taking up space on, finding nothing.

What the fuck?

Then I see it. The little white piece of paper.

Reed,
Thank you. Talk soon.
♡ Athena

"What the motherfuck is this shit?" I shout to the empty room.

She left?

Thank you?

This better be a motherfucking misunderstanding.

Enraged, I storm downstairs to the parking lot. Her car's gone.

I'm stunned stupid.

Next stop's Dante's door. His bike was in the parking lot, so I hope to fuck he's here.

He answers breathless and shirtless and I don't give one fuck what I might have interrupted.

"What?" he snaps.

"Where is she?" I'm too crazed to even form a more complete sentence.

"Who?"

"Athena."

"How the fuck would I know?"

Karina's voice drifts through the crack in the door, and I shove it open all the way. She's scrambling into a T-shirt and I'm so fucked in the head, I can't even appreciate the brief glimpse at her naked rack.

Dante knocks me out of the room with a hand to my chest. A second later, Karina scurries around him.

"What'd she say?" she asks.

"Nothing. She left me a fuckin' note." I hand it to her and she reads it quickly.

"Oh, shit. I didn't think she was still going."

"Going where?" Dante asks before I get a chance.

Karina bites her lip and glances up at Dante as if asking for protection from my rage.

"Los Angeles," she finally answers.

"What?" She could have said Mars for all the sense that makes to me.

"She wants to be an actress—"

"You knew about this?" I shout as I take a step closer.

Dante's meaty hand is back at my chest, stopping me from getting any closer to Karina. "Watch yourself, fucker. Yell at her again, and I'll tear your head off," he says in a smooth, even voice that does little to calm me down.

Karina's got inner strength, because even though I'm raging like a bull, she steps up and looks me in the eye. "She just told me about this plan of hers a few weeks ago. She supposedly has an apartment lined up—"

"What?" I hate how raw and hoarse my voice comes out, but I just spent fuck knows how many days with Athena and she never mentioned any of this.

"Babe, go call her," Dante says, and Karina steps back inside the room.

"Sorry, brother. I didn't know."

"It's going right to voicemail," Karina says when she returns, the phone pressed to her ear. She looks up at me with apologetic eyes. "I've been telling her for days to talk to you about it."

"She went by herself? Does she even know anyone there?" Dante asks.

"I don't know. She told me she found her roommate on Craigslist. I warned her it sounded like a bad idea."

"Jesus Christ, she could be meeting up with anyone," I grumble. "Why didn't you talk her out of it?"

"I tried, but Athena's pretty headstrong when she wants to be," Karina answers calmly.

Dante nudges her inside their room. "Go wait on the bed." Great. How thrilling, my fucked-up situation can be an excuse for him to spank her ass or whatever kinky shit the two of them get into.

He steps out into the hall and shuts the door. "What do you want to do?"

I know he's asking if I want his help going after her.

Fuck that.

"Nothing," I say, straightening my shoulders. "It was just a fuck. Doesn't mean shit. Just woulda been nice to have a head's up so I could replace her."

Dante shakes his head. I'm not fooling him.

I'm not fooling myself either.

ELEVEN

ATHENA

TEARS RUN down my cheeks almost the entire trip to Los Angeles. Why? Why can't I stop crying? I left of my own free will.

My phone blows up about two hours into my trip. *Karina.* I shut the phone off and keep driving.

What Google Maps told me was a five-hour and fifty-five minute trip, ends up taking me eight hours. The traffic at this hour is ridiculous. I end up driving around the street ten times before I see the small entrance to the parking space behind my building.

The apartment's a lot seedier than it looked in the ads.

The neighborhood's supposed to be decent. The rent's certainly high enough. It's close to my acting classes so that I can walk there. The first pang of excitement hits me.

I made it.

I'm here.

You've been waiting your whole life for this.

Is Reed upset that I left?

All those little whispered thoughts go through my mind as I stare at the building. My new home.

My excitement gets snuffed out when I enter our building. Our apartment is on the second floor. The door is wide open and people seem to be coming and going. I'm exhausted and just want to sleep, not deal with a bunch of strangers.

"Roxanne?" I ask, poking my head inside.

"Ohmygod!" a short blonde shouts and hurries over. "Athena! You're finally here. I was about to rent your room out to someone else."

That better be a joke. I'm paid up for the month.

"Everyone, this is my new roomie, Athena. Be nice." Most of the people she introduces me to are around my age. Under the pounds of makeup caked on her face, I figure Roxanne, or Roxy as she insists I call her, to be around twenty-two or twenty-three.

She shows me to my room, which is miraculously clean and quiet, given the party going on in the living room.

"You gonna crash?" she asks from the doorway.

"Yeah. Sorry. It was a long drive."

"Okay. I'm about ready to kick some of these fuckers out anyway."

"Thanks."

"We'll chat in the morning and I'll show you around."

"Sounds good."

I close the door and I'm relieved to find an extra lock on it. After sliding it into place, I strip and dig out Romeo's T-shirt to sleep in. It smells like him and today hits me like a bag of nickels to the face. What the fuck did I do? I really like him. Maybe...

I convinced myself I'd see him when I go home for the Fourth, but by then he'll probably have moved on to one of those girls in his club and forgotten about me. And if I'd given up on my dream for him and then he dumped me later, I'd be furious with myself.

Besides, how was a long-distance relationship between us really going to work? Was he going to ride out here every weekend to see me? Would he insist I come home?

You didn't even give him a chance to figure it out.

"Shut up," I mutter to myself like a crazy person.

I pull out a set of clean sheets, and not trusting Roxy's housekeeping skills, make the bed.

Big day tomorrow.

TWELVE

ROMEO

AFTER A WEEK of drinking and generally being a dick to everyone in sight, I still can't stop picturing *her* every time I try to go to sleep. Those steel-blue eyes haunt me every god damn time I close my eyes.

Wolf pounds me on the back on his way into church. "You're pathetic."

"Fuck off."

"You need to get laid," Whip says.

Is everyone planning to give me shit today?

"Melody brought one of her friends with her," Cricket suggests. He just got voted in, so no, I'm not real receptive to dating advice from the little punk.

"Worry about your own dick," I snarl.

"Just tryin' to help, Prez."

No shit. Getting someone else underneath me *would* probably help me move on, but I can't be bothered. My dick must be broken, because he's not interested either.

Once I'm seated at the head of the table, some of the

fog lifts and I finally concentrate on something besides her.

Wolf raises his hand. "We got word that one, Red Storm's trying to move into Dragon territory. And two, they're patching in LEOs now."

A round of what-the-fucks go around the table. If Red Storm's being infiltrated by law enforcement, that could be bad for all the MCs in the area.

Dante sits forward. "How reliable?"

Wolf puts his hand up and wobbles it back and forth. "Too early to tell."

"Who gives a fuck then?" Dante asks.

"Hey, just passing along information."

"This info come from Tucker?"

"Yeah."

"Is Bolt asking us for help with pushing them out of their territory?" I ask.

"Not yet."

"Good. Then Dante's right. Not our problem." Tucker going into Red Storm territory to gather information still bugs me, though. Yeah, he said it was to help right the wrong done to his daughter, but he's also a known liar. "Just to be safe. I say we reroute our next shipment through Nevada and have Fang truck it instead of Tucker."

"Works for me," Dante agrees. Everyone else gives their yeses.

We go through a list of less-exciting club business. There's a surprising amount of tedious paperwork involved in running a successful outlaw motorcycle club. Any bunch of assholes can call a building a clubhouse and play outlaw biker. To survive and succeed at it takes some skill, hard work, and cunning. All my brothers have those qualities or they wouldn't be wearing the Iron Bulls patch. For the first time, *I'm* the one not pulling my weight because I'm fucked up over a chick. It pisses me the fuck off.

When we break, I stay behind to talk to Wolf and go through some papers. Once I'm satisfied I've done some actual work, I join my brothers in the common area.

Ignoring the degenerate acts going on around me, I spot Dante and his girl at the bar with Luck. No, I will not go over there and casually ask if she's heard from Athena. I don't give a shit.

Against my better judgment, I approach the bar. Karina gives me a look that's part fear and part pity. I hate that I lost my shit in front of her the other day. Hate that I let her see how much her little friend got under my skin.

Aware that it's completely unreasonable to blame Karina for my misery, I can't help the annoyance that creeps over me when she's near. So I ignore her completely.

Luck passes me a Jack and Coke before I open my mouth. Probably for the best, otherwise something stupid's about to roll off my tongue. Dante waits until I'm a few rounds in to needle me.

"Prez, you must be, what, ninety percent alcohol by now?" he asks with a smug face I'd love to punch if I didn't think I'd miss and hit the wooden pillar behind him.

Luck has more respect for his president than Dante does and asks if I want to switch to soda.

"No," I snap at Luck. Then I turn my pissed-offedness on Dante. *He's* the one I should really blame. Asshole just had to hook up with some chick with a friend. Never mind if girls didn't bring their friends by, we'd have the same tired pussy day after day. I'm not in a logical mood or making sense at the moment. "Fuck off," I spit at Dante, without turning my head.

He laughs. In what's left of my peripheral vision, I spot Karina shaking her head at him. Christ, I don't need a girl trying to stick up for me.

That's the last straw. I stay here much longer, I'm bound to throw a punch or say something mean to Karina and I'm in no condition to defend myself from Dante's sledge-hammer sized fists.

Even worse, the longer I'm around Karina, I'm afraid I'll cave and ask if she's heard from Athena.

No. Not happening.

Leaning over the bar, I snag an unopened bottle of Jack Daniels, and let my middle finger fly at everyone in the room.

Drunk and alone, I take my sorry ass upstairs.

Athena

Stupid little girl.

I've been called that more than once during my first week in Los Angeles.

It wouldn't be so annoying if it wasn't true.

Every day it becomes more and more clear how pathetically underprepared I am. Hollywood isn't glamorous. It's hard work, dead ends, and mean people.

The whole myth about being "discovered" is just a myth, I'm finding out. It's hard to be discovered in a place where every town in America seems to have sent their two most beautiful people.

I'll never forgive myself if I don't return Karina's dozens of calls. Surprisingly, she hasn't mentioned Romeo at all. She does let me vent for a long time, though.

"Tall, pretty blondes are everywhere. I'm one of thousands. Not only that, but most of them have been auditioning for commercials, or enrolled in theater schools since they were kids. They've got experience working on sets in small roles that I never even knew existed. They've worked for nothing in projects like student films, experimental plays, short films, showcases... I don't even know where to look to find the non-paying roles, let alone the paying ones."

I stop and take a breath, and her laughter comes over the line. "You're so brave."

"I'm an idiot."

"Well, that too."

Before I chicken out, I blurt out the question I've been dying to ask. "How's Romeo?"

She's silent for a minute. "He...he wasn't happy."

"Really? But it was just a fling. He must have girls in and out of his bed all the time."

Even over the line, I sense her irritation. "Yes, but he really seemed to like *you*. I haven't known him that long, but he seemed different with you. Now he's back to being a nasty jerk."

"Sorry."

She's not done making me feel like shit though. "You were the first girl I saw him with more than once."

"Ew."

"Shut up. You know what I mean. I've never seen him get upset over a girl leaving either."

He was upset? "Should I call him?"

"Maybe. You should've talked to him before you left. I think leaving a *note* pissed him off the most."

Shame washes over me. That was a shitty, cowardly thing to do. "He showed it to you?"

"Yes. *Thank you?* Really?"

"Well, you know my parents always insisted I write a thank you note."

She chuckles. "Yes, princess, but I don't think a thanks-for-taking-my-virginity-note was what they had in mind."

See, I *am* a stupid little girl. "I didn't know what to do," I admit miserably.

"Obviously. Are you still coming home for the Fourth?"

"Maybe."

She sighs. We talk a little longer and then hang up.

I didn't want to tell her the reason I hesitated about coming home is because gas is crazy-expensive. Wait. Make that, *everything* is expensive. Luxuries like road trips home might have to be put on hold. After only a few days out here, I realized if I didn't find a job I'd run through my cushion of money fast.

Guess what? The thousands of other wannabe actors stuffed into this city already have jobs. No one wants to hire an eighteen-year-old girl with no experience. At least

I have my high school diploma, one person told me. It put me in the top fifty percent of the pile.

Yay, me.

It's embarrassing how big of a mistake I made.

I keep telling myself I'm on the right track. I've readjusted my expectations—more than once. I'm enrolled in a class with a great acting coach. Although, on the first day he told us "You can never control the opportunities, but you can control the readiness." Those words hit my stomach like a mule's hoof.

I'm not ready for any of this.

I really am the stupid little girl everyone keeps saying I am.

"Honey, L.A. is a cruel bitch. She will spit you out and send you back to whence you came if you do *not* come to her one hundred percent committed," my new friend, Elliot, says with a lot of head shaking and finger wagging, when I explain my plans to him after our How to Audition class. He's the first person, besides Roxy and my acting coach, who hasn't either ignored me or insulted me.

"I thought I *was* committed."

"They all think that."

"Thanks."

He asks if I want to go out and insists I should be dating too. But my heart isn't in it.

"Is it a guy? Tell me it's about a guy."

"Sort of. I started something before I came out here and just up and left." Good God, it sounds even worse when I say it out loud.

"I want to hear everything."

I don't have a chance because as we walk into my apartment, it's clear it's one of *those* nights. Roxy's entertaining a number of her rough-looking friends again. Some of them wear vests with patches, similar to Romeo's, so it makes me miss him even more. These guys are nothing like Romeo and Dante, though. While yes, Romeo's pretty crude, I never felt unsafe around him. Quite the opposite.

These guys, though? They're more like boys pretending to be hardened men, instead of actual men.

Elliot hesitates inside the door.

"Who's the queer, Athena?" the least charming of the bunch, Snake, calls out.

The guys catcall and make a bunch of nasty comments, and my cheeks burn with shame. I don't want Elliot to think these are the kind of people I associate with.

"Uh, these are my roommate's friends," I tell him, too embarrassed to look him in the eye.

He seems to acknowledge that with a single nod. "I'm gonna go, honey. I don't care for the way Miss Congeniality over there keeps staring at me," he says, indicating Snake.

"I'll go with you."

When we're outside, I offer a lame apology, but Elliot stops me.

"Are you sure you're safe there? It looks like one big STD petri dish going on."

I snort at the joke because I've had similar thoughts. No judgment, but Roxy gets around. Good for her and all, but the guys are sleazy and treat her like crap, so I don't understand the appeal.

"Yeah, none of them bother me."

"Well, if it ever gets bad, don't hesitate to come over. I've got a couch and you're welcomed to it anytime."

"Thanks." My eyes well up and Elliot shakes his head. "Save that for the camera, honey."

"Oh, shit. We're supposed to be at rehearsal."

Elliot had gotten me my first "role." Had I not listened carefully the first day of class, I would have laughed when his friend offered me the part. It pays nothing and the rehearsal time has been significant, considering how little I'm on stage.

It's fun, though. And I'm getting experience and hopefully someone will see me in it and maybe offer me a bigger non-paying role.

One can only hope, right?

THIRTEEN
ROMEO

"Hi, it's Athena. I wanted to talk...explain..."

My thumb hovers over the "delete" button. I end up hitting "save," because fuck it feels good to hear her voice.

She can fuck right off, though, if she thinks I'm calling her back.

I reached down, strapped on my balls, and threw myself into work at the garage this week. Turns out to be a good thing because with summer here, we've got more cars than mechanics and fabricators. My shop has a reputation for transforming clunkers into show-quality classics one bolt at a time. Right now, we're backed up and the fourteen to sixteen hour work days give me the perfect distraction.

Thank fuck I never brought her to my garage like I'd been planning.

"Yo, boss," one of my mechanics calls out. "Greyson has a '76 vette he wants to unload. It's in rough shape. You want it for a project car?"

Fuck me. I just can't catch a break, can I? I finally got her off my fucking mind, and then the car she told me she wants shows up at my shop? Seriously? What did I do to piss off the universe?

For some idiotic reason, I say yes to the car.

Goddammit. It's even red.

I'm exhausted and annoyed when I drag my ass into the clubhouse. After days of being reminded of her every time I look around my clubhouse, I've come to fully appreciate the wisdom of having a home away from here like Dante, Luck, and some of the other brothers have. Returning to my empty room night after night sucks.

The camera I used to film us the last time we fucked taunts me from my dresser. I haven't bothered to watch it. What's the point? I plug the card into my laptop, just for a brief preview.

My dick throws a tantrum behind my fly when she comes on the screen. I'm iron-hard for the first time in a while, watching her move and tease. Before I even realize it, my dick's in my hand and I'm giving it long slow strokes. When on-screen-Athena puts her mouth on my cock, my hips jerk remembering that phantom tongue. Pissed as hell that all I have left is a fucking video.

I barely have time to grab a towel before my body seizes. But it's just a meaningless release. Physically, I feel calmer. Everywhere else, I'm only more agitated.

From the screen she still torments me, until I shut the computer down.

If only shutting down my brain were as simple.

Athena

Roxy isn't a completely awful roommate. When it's just the two of us, and not her posse of thuggish biker-poser boyfriends, she's actually fun.

Today she's helpful too.

"I have a lead on an audition in Beachwood if you want it. I can't go."

I haven't really figured out what Roxy does. She says she goes on auditions, but mostly she seems to party and hang out. As long as her half of the rent gets paid, I suppose it's none of my business.

"What's it for?"

"Some sort of reality thing."

Beachwood's too far to walk, so I reluctantly take my car out of its space and fight my way through traffic.

The neighborhood—when I finally find the place—is decent enough.

It turns weird when I'm called into the audition room, though. There's a cheap table and chair set up across from a spacious black leather couch. Two guys and two video cameras.

One of the forms they ask me to fill out asks a bunch of medical questions. Since I'm still new at this, I don't know if that's normal or not.

A nervous fluttering starts up in my belly but I tamp it down.

The two guys are nice enough. They invite me to sit on the couch and one of them casually flicks the camera on. They ask me to pull out my identification and hold it up to my face to take a picture. They're real focused on whether I'm actually eighteen.

Some inner voice tells me to *run*.

"So are you comfortable with nudity?" Creep number one—as I've now named him in my head for asking that question—slides his slimy gaze up and down my body. "You've got a nice frame. Very well-proportioned."

"Um—"

Creep number two picks up where his skeevy buddy left off. "You're in Hollywood, babe. You can't get work unless you get naked."

Luckily, Elliot and my acting coach warned me about this sort of thing.

"What is this for again?" I ask.

"A film," creep number one answers vaguely.

Creep number two adds, "Come on, every girl your age has had sex on camera."

My cheeks heat up remembering the video Romeo and I made together. But that was sexy, fun, and somehow… sweet. I was excited and felt safe.

Here, I feel sick and scared.

"This is a mistake." I get up and grab my bag. Creep number one moves in front of the door.

"We really think you've got potential, Athena." I hate that I told these two jerks my real name and that they have a copy of my license.

"I'm not feeling very well." It's not a lie either. I'm about to throw up if I don't get out of here.

They try a few more times to convince me to stay but finally realize it's not happening. In the hallway, two nervous girls wait anxiously for their turn.

"It's a porn audition," I warn them.

"We know. Anal Angels Seventeen," they whoop and giggle like it's the greatest thing ever.

I'm going to kill Roxy.

FOURTEEN

ATHENA

"How'd you do?" Roxy asks when I return to the apartment a couple hours later.

"It was for a porno."

She makes this *so what* face, and it hits me that she knew *exactly* what I'd be walking into.

"I didn't come out here to do porn," I explain as calmly as possible.

"Seriously? They pay like a thousand dollars a scene. I thought you were looking for a job."

"Yeah, I was thinking more like waiting tables, not taking strange dick up my ass."

"Oh! They pay *way* more for anal."

I stand there blinking because I have no response to that. None. Nope. My words have left my brain.

"No."

"Okay." She shrugs. "Sorry. I was just trying to help."

She follows me into the kitchen and watches while I put a salad together for dinner. "Do you want half?" I ask.

"No. Snake's bringing pizza over."

Great. Guess I'll be spending my evening hiding out in my room.

At least this time Snake only shows up with two of his shifty-looking buddies.

After dinner, I point to his vest and ask about the patches.

He raises an eyebrow as if I've finally said something worthwhile. "You know something about MCs, Athena?"

"No. Not really. My best friend lives with a guy in one, and I've hung out with them." What am I supposed to do, give this jerk the whole stupid story?

"She his ol' lady?" Roxy asks.

"No. She's my age."

All four of them have a good laugh at that.

When Roxy stops giggling like a brain dead Barbie, she explains. "No. It's like wife status in an MC."

"Oh."

Oh shit.

When I asked Reed how he knew Karina's father, he said something about old ladies. *Old ladies stay out of club business.* Did he mean he wanted me to be—

"Athena?"

"What?"

"I was saying be careful. I got booted out of a club back in New York for not kissing the ass of the president's ol' lady. Hardcore MC guys take that shit seriously."

"Well, she's my best friend, so it's not an issue."

She shrugs. "I'm just saying. That's why I like Snake being a nomad. I don't have to worry about that shit."

He chuckles, a dark hollow sort of laugh that gives me the chills.

When I can slip out of the room without them noticing, I do. I'm exhausted and confused. Overwhelmed. I miss Romeo. I feel awful for leaving the way I did. Maybe we could have tried long-distance, or I could have enrolled in acting classes back home.

Now, I'll never know.

Like an idiot, I try calling him again. He's ignored every one of my other fifty phone calls. I'm not sure why I think this time will be any different.

Yup, straight to voicemail.

"It's me again. I know you don't want to talk to me. But I wanted to say I miss you."

That's so pathetic. I wish I could hack into his voicemail and erase it. Hopefully he deletes my messages without listening to them.

I try Karina, and at least she answers my calls.

"What's up?"

"Nothing. My roommate sent me on a porn audition today."

"Oh my God. You didn't."

"Ew. Of course not. I got the hell out of there."

Her warm laughter eases the ickiness that followed me home from the casting couch. I haven't gone this long without seeing my best friend since we met and I miss her terribly.

"Everything else okay?" she asks.

"No. I don't know. Roxy has her shady boyfriend and his friends here again."

"Athena, I wish you'd find another roommate."

"I know. I'm not on the lease, so I could leave, but that's a shitty thing to do."

"You're too nice."

"Hey, are you Dante's old lady?"

She chuckles. "I guess. It's not official, in the eyes of the club yet. There's a special—never mind. What made you ask that?"

"Roxy said something about it."

"Be careful what you say about the club to strangers, Athena. Seriously."

"I will. I didn't use any names or anything."

"Good. She sounds shady as hell."

I sigh and yawn. "I've got an early class, so I'm going to try to get some sleep."

"Got your earplugs?"

"Yup." I'd told her Roxy and Snake had woken me from a dead sleep more than once with their loud, raunchy sex antics.

Feeling lonely, I slip into Romeo's shirt. It's starting to smell more like me than him, but it still makes me feel better.

THE NEXT MORNING, I'm up before anyone else and I'm in the kitchen making coffee when Snake startles me.

"Iron Bulls? That's who your friend's hooked up with?"

"Shit!" Coffee grounds go flying all over the kitchen, and I stop to sweep them up before answering. "You startled me."

He seems completely unconcerned and appears to be waiting for me to answer his question.

"Yeah."

"Who's she with?"

"Uh, their Sergeant whatever?"

He grunts as an answer, but when I turn around, he spots the lettering on the front of my shirt. "You hook up with their prez?"

What an obnoxious asshole. "No." My red cheeks say otherwise, though, and he nods slowly.

"Where's Roxy?"

He gives me a sly smile that's creepy as hell. "Still sleepin'."

"Oh. Well, I have to get ready for class, so I'll get out of your way."

Screw it. I'd rather spend my last seventy-five cents on a day-old bagel for breakfast than spend any more time around Snake.

Romeo

I almost picked up the phone last night. Her *"I wanted to say I miss you"* message definitely fucked with my head. In fact, the memory of her voice chased me downstairs to the bar at ten in the morning, instead of where I should be —the garage.

"Can I talk to you?" Karina's soft voice pulls me away from my thoughts.

Not sure what the fuck she's doing here this early in the morning. I glance over and find her fidgeting "Dante ain't here," I snap.

"I know. I stopped by to talk to *you*." A slight note of

exasperation colors her voice. I find that funny, since most of the time she seems so reserved.

"What's on your mind?"

I didn't have to ask. I already know it has something to do with her friend. It's not like we have much else to talk about.

"I'm worried about Athena."

Shit. I thought maybe she was going to try to talk me into answering Athena's calls or calling her back. "Why?"

She reacts to my sharp tone by taking a step back and I fight back the urge to shake her.

"Her roommate sounds sketchy. She sent her on an audition for a porn—"

"What?" I barely keep my voice below a shout.

"She left the audition. But it's more than that. The girl has these shady bikers hanging out there all the time."

I'm not liking the sound of any of this. Yeah, I'm pissed at Athena, but I don't want her to get hurt. "She say which club?"

Karina shakes her head. "No. Do you want me to ask next time?"

"Yeah. Find out for me. Give me the address too."

Why do I care? Why am I inserting myself into Athena's life when she so clearly doesn't want me to be a part of it?

She's called you fifty times, jackass.

I really ain't in the mood for my conscience to play devil's advocate.

Karina scribbles out the address and hands it over. "Thank you. I've been worried about it all night and

Dante's not home, or I would have talked to him, but Luck said I should tell you," she babbles out.

"Yeah. You did the right thing." Since I've been a bit of an asshole to her, it took some guts to bring this to me by herself. She's a loyal girl, something I respect. "Thanks, Karina."

Athena

I landed a real audition. It's hard to explain this sort of milestone to anyone but another actor, so I end up celebrating with Elliot. He's beside himself excited for me.

The role is "slutty waitress." Yes, that's the description. It's non-union, background work. But it's a real television pilot and Elliot assures me it's a big deal.

I don't get the part.

But it's still huge, and we go out to celebrate anyway.

"Pamela Parker casts a lot of other shows, Athena. She was impressed with you. I bet she'll call you next time she's looking for someone. We need to find you a manager."

"What would I have done if you didn't take me under your wing?"

He chuckles. "I guess you'd be taking it up the ass out in Beachwood."

"Jerk." I slap his shoulder. "I never should have told you about that."

"No. It's mandatory you tell me these things. I need it as a cautionary tale for the next young starlet who stumbles into town."

I hadn't thought of it like that.

"You don't know how many girls would have gone through with it. I'm really proud of you for sticking to your guns."

A sad sniffle escapes me. "Thanks."

He walks me home, but ever since Roxy's friends hassled him, he's refused to come upstairs. I don't blame him and I still burn with shame every time I remember the incident.

For the first time since I moved here, I seem to be alone in the apartment.

After a few seconds of unnatural silence, my gaze skips around the room. Television, dvd player, speakers—all gone. The one working lamp in the living room is also missing. I flick on the weak overhead light to get a better look.

Were we robbed?

Is Roxy hurt? I hurry into her bedroom and find everything personal missing. Right down to the sheets. Photographs, clothes, shoes, all of it—gone.

She ditched me?

Panic turns my stomach inside out. What the fuck am I going to do? There's no way I can afford this place by myself. I yank out my phone to call Elliot when the front door slams open.

"Roxy?" I yell as I run out to the living room. I'm so gonna kick her skinny ass—

Not Roxy.

Snake struts through the door like he owns the place. Two of his friends follow him. I've only met them one other time and never bothered to learn their names since they creeped me out so much.

This is bad. Why doesn't this apartment have a back door? Or a fire escape? Why did I have to find my roommate on Craigslist for fuck's sake?

"Uh hey, Snake. Roxy's gone. Looks like she took off and stuck me with the apartment," I explain, hoping he'll leave.

Instead he turns his fiery eyes my way. I don't know what he's so pissed about, but I have a feeling I'm about to find out.

"She skipped town because she stole a package and a lotta cash from me," he says slowly, lacing each word with venom.

"I, uh, don't know anything about that."

"Mind if we search your place?" he asks as he stalks closer. I don't get the impression saying *no* is one of my options, so I bob my head up and down. His friends are already busy tearing apart the living room. So much for getting our security deposit back. Maybe if they search and see nothing's here, they'll give up and go away.

And maybe while they're busy searching, I can slip out the door.

No such luck. Snake wraps his hand around my arm and asks me to "help" him.

Those drunk little bees start buzzing in my stomach, telling me it's time to get the hell out of here. Except, I can't seem to shake his iron grip on my arm.

The prick even insists on searching my room.

"Roxy never comes in here."

He snorts. "That's what you think."

That little bitch.

He stops at the cardboard box I've been using as a

nightstand and picks up a picture of Karina and I before prom. "Who's this?"

His sharp tone makes me flinch and I really don't like the unnatural interest he's taking in the photo. "That's my friend from back home."

He raises one dark eyebrow. "The ol' lady?"

God that sounds silly. "Yes."

His beady eyes run over the photograph for a moment longer. Why, I have no clue. "How much you think you're worth to her?" he asks as he shoves me on my bed.

I bounce right up into a sitting position. "What?"

He blocks my escape with his body. Looming over me, but not touching, thank God. "Seems like you got a connection to the Iron Bulls. Think their prez will pay for you?"

He won't even take a phone call from me. "No."

"Why? You a bad lay?"

We're moving into territory I don't want to discuss with this creep.

When I don't answer, he laughs again. "I hope not. Now that Roxy's gone, I'm gonna need someone to replace her."

"I'm sure plenty of women will be happy to…take care of you."

He grins as if I paid him a compliment. "What's wrong, baby? You ain't interested? Roxy said you're real uptight. Maybe *my* snake can help you with that."

Eww.

My lips press into a thin line and my refusal to take the bait seems to piss him off. His fingers wrap into my hair and he yanks me off the bed, forcing me to the floor.

Every inch of me trembles in fear. I swear, if he puts his little *snake* anywhere near my mouth, I'm biting it.

Dammit. Instead of all the acting classes, I should have signed up for a self-defense class.

"Where's your phone?" he asks.

It's in my back pocket and I'd kind of been hoping he'd leave so I could pull it out and call for help.

But I guess he'd be one hell of a lousy bad guy if he let that happen.

"Listen, bitch. You can either hand it to me so I can call your boyfriend—"

"He's not my boyfriend and he won't answer if it's me."

Doubt flashes over his face, then anger. His hold on my hair tightens and he gives me a shake. "Don't interrupt, bitch. Give me your phone." He raises his eyebrows like a cartoon perv, "Or I'll call my friends in and the three of us will search your body until we find it."

Somehow I'd managed to forget all about the two goons searching the rest of the apartment. My hand slides into my back pocket and I reluctantly hand over my phone.

He immediately starts scrolling through it. "Ka-ree-nah," he mumbles and his face lights up in a disgusting smirk. "Hot little bitch," he mutters.

I'd hate myself for possibly endangering my best friend, but Dante will keep her safe. It's obvious he'd murder anyone who hurt her. It reminds me of how fiercely Romeo protected me from the guard he thought was a threat at the music festival.

After the thoughtless way I left him, there's no way he's going to cough up a dime to rescue me. And I don't blame him. Snake will make his demands. Romeo will laugh and hang up. Then I'll be at the mercy of Snake and his friends. A fitting ending for a girl whose list of stupid things she's done keeps growing and growing.

Snake pockets my phone then glances up and catches me trying to crawl away. It's a pitiful effort, really. I mean, where the hell am I supposed to go? His boot lands on my chest. Not a kick, but a forceful nudge back into place.

He whips out a bunch of zip ties. Figures this lowlife carries a stash of kidnapping supplies hidden in his cargo pants pockets. When he secures me to the metal frame of the bed, I'm ashamed to say, I'm too scared to fight hard. Afraid he'll hurt me worse if I don't cooperate.

"Stay put." He snickers on his way out. The door slams shut behind him, leaving me in my dimly lit bedroom. While I'm distressed about my predicament, I'm also relieved that he left me alone.

A few minutes later he returns. *Damn.*

"Yeah. She's fine for now." He flips on a light and points my phone to snap a photo of my pathetic self, helplessly tied to the bed frame. The light goes off and the doors shuts again.

I catch bits and pieces of the phone call. The phrase "skull fuck your bitch" comes through the thin door, clear enough that I'm properly frightened.

Did Romeo actually answer the phone? A small glimmer of hope flutters in my chest. Maybe he doesn't hate me so much that he'll leave me to get raped and murdered by this psycho.

What seems like hours later, Snake pokes his head in the door. "You must be a better fuck than you think.

President Romeo's on his way and gave his word he's bringing a rack of dead presidents to buy your sweet ass."

I'll need a month to unpack that sentence. My takeaway—Romeo's coming to save me, and I weep with relief.

FIFTEEN

ROMEO

"Motherfucker!"

Everyone in the clubhouse turns and stares.

I jab my finger in the direction of the open chapel door. "Chapel. Now. Everyone."

Dante walks in the clubhouse as brothers hustle into the other room.

It doesn't take a genius to see how tightly wound I am. "What's wrong, Prez?" he asks.

"I know you just got back, but I need you."

"Yeah. Okay. Right behind you."

That's how this club, our brotherhood, works. Not because I'm the president. It would be this way for any of us. One brother says he needs something, we have each other's backs.

And right now I really appreciate that loyalty. I'm gonna need it when I explain this fucked-up situation.

I barely make it inside the room without losing it. I can't sit. "I got a call from some nomad motherfucker who's got Athena. Says he's gonna hurt her if I don't bring him money."

Dante explodes out of his chair, ready to leave right now. "Jesus, fuck. Are you serious? Is she okay?"

"Are you sure this isn't a setup?" Wolf asks.

Just because we have each other's backs, doesn't mean the fuckers won't ask some pointed questions. "No," I answer evenly before sending the picture of *Athena tied to a bed* to everyone at the table. Thinking about the slimy piece of shit I spoke to on the phone touching Athena, has me shaking with rage.

"Yeah, but she could be in on it," Stryker says.

"This the bitch who up and left you?" Whip asks.

"It doesn't fucking matter," I snap. "They snatched her because of her connection to me. This isn't club business. It's personal, so if you don't want to get involved, that's fine."

Whip and Stryker exchange a glance.

"Athena wouldn't do that," Cricket pipes up. "I'll ride with you, Prez."

Dante's already pulling cash out of the safe, so I think it's pretty clear where he stands. Since he's got the personality of a pissed off polar bear most of the time, and doesn't give two fucks about many people, my brothers start treating this as more than my own personal piece-of-ass-problem. Since there's a six-hour ride ahead of us, I ain't got time to waste being offended.

Our treasurer, Stryker, helps Dante count and package the money.

"Wolf, Stryker, I need you two to stay here and hold things down."

Whip seems to be more on board now. "I'll go plan the route. Got an address?"

"Yeah."

"How many in his crew?" Luck asks.

"Don't know. Heard at least one other guy in the background."

"Karina said Athena mentioned three guys regularly hanging around there," he offers.

Whip barely glances away from his laptop. "Makes sense. He's a nomad, he ain't gonna be rolling with too many."

Fifteen minutes later I'm on the road with five of my brothers. In case one of us breaks down or we need to cart a body back, two prospects follow behind us in a van. Whip leads us on what he says is the quickest route and even though he pissed me off back at the table, I trust his judgment.

We make one stop outside Los Angeles, so I can call the little punk holding Athena and let him know we're close.

"Yeah, man. Me and your girl are just chillin'. She's a sweet little thing. Seems sort of shy, but maybe I can work that out of her if you don't get here soon."

Even though I'm seething inside, I don't react to his taunt. "We'll be there in about an hour."

I lied. We're there in twenty minutes. I want the extra time to map out the area. See how busy it is. Assess if it's the type of neighborhood where folks call the cops every time they hear a gunshot.

It's not a South Central ghetto. But it sure as fuck ain't the sort of place a girl like Athena should be living.

It burns my ass she left me to live in a dump like this, when I would have given her anything and everything she needed.

Not that she had any reason to know that, since in the short time we spent together, all I did was find new and inventive ways to stick my dick in her.

Fuck it. All I care about now is getting her out of here safely and then getting the fuck away from her.

The door that corresponds to the number Snake gave me sits busted open. I assume he did that. The thought of him terrorizing Athena heats my blood to the point I'm liable to snap and kill this motherfucker the minute I see him.

Dante and Nero follow behind me.

The two pansies pretending to guard the living room almost piss themselves when we enter.

"Snake?"

One of the pansies points to the hallway.

Dante steps up. "You got two seconds to get the fuck out of here."

They don't need two seconds.

So much for loyalty and brotherhood. Dante glances at me and smirks.

"You got this?" I ask and he nods.

The apartment's silent. What if they moved her somewhere else?

Then Snake calls out for one of his guys. When no one answers, he steps into the living room. The cocky smirk on his face falters when he gets a good look at me and my crew. Not one of *my* brothers will leave me to fend for myself.

"Your friends left," Dante says, answering Snake's unspoken question.

"Where's Athena?" I ask.

Snake slides his arrogant smile back on. "Chill, Prez. She's fine." He waves his hands around in a thuggish *calm down, bro* gesture. This motherfucker better enjoy his last few moments of having four fully functioning limbs.

"Where's my money?" Snake asks.

Dante glances at me and I nod. Even though I haven't spotted a weapon on Snake yet, I want to do this as clean as possible.

Dante throws the duffle bag of cash at the prick, who digs through it like a fat kid with his sack of Halloween candy. Too stupid to realize he's outnumbered and we've got no reason to keep him alive, Snake points down the hallway. "Your girl's down there, Prez. Waitin' for ya."

I trust Dante to take care of the situation and leave to go find my girl.

The first door I encounter is open a crack and I push it wider, hand on my weapon in case of surprises. But all I find is my girl huddled on the floor, hands laced tight together and then tied to the bed restraining her from moving far.

She lifts her head and the tear tracks all over her face push me forward.

Down on both knees, I whip out the pocketknife I carry at all times, and cut her loose.

I take her face between my hands, checking for any damage. Shit, she's more beautiful than I remember. Even all dirty and teary.

She throws her arms around me, almost knocking me over.

A rush of air leaves my lungs. "You're okay, sweetheart."

"Thank you. Thank you," she says over and over. "I'm so sorry. I can't believe you came."

Now isn't the time to talk about how this doesn't mean there's anything between us, so I don't.

She scrunches her face and wriggles around. "I need to pee. He wouldn't let me up. Told me to piss myself."

I help her up and to the bathroom and then join Dante and the others in the living room, where Dante's working Snake over with his massive fists.

"Save something for me, brother."

Dante glances up and all but snarls at me. He's way into kill mode here. "Snake. He's the one Tucker hired." He barely sounds human uttering the words, but I get what he's saying.

I hold up a hand to stop Dante for a second. "You're on the run from the Red Storm, right?" I ask Snake.

Behind me, the bathroom door opens. "Go back in the bedroom and stay there, Athena."

Thankfully, she doesn't argue. After she's safely shut inside the bedroom, I nod at Snake who thrusts his defiant chin up. "I ain't on the run from no one."

"That's not what I heard."

He shakes his head and drops of blood splatter on the already filthy carpet. "Your bitch's roommate stole from me. Just gettin' my money back. Leave my club out of it."

The angrier I am inside, the calmer I appear outside. I lean back against the wall and cross my arms over my chest. "You know Athena had nothing to do with that. And maybe you haven't heard, but there's a nice fat reward for your half-dead carcass."

His eyes widen because he knows I'm speaking the truth.

I glance at Dante. "Athena doesn't need to see this. Take him to the back bedroom. Do what you gotta do. But don't kill him. Deacon wants him alive."

While Dante drags Snake to the back of the apartment, Nero cleans things up in the living room. I leave to get Athena.

She's busy jamming things into a backpack when I walk in the bedroom, but stops as soon as she sees me.

Rushing over, she throws her arms around me. "Thank you so much. I'm so—"

I cut her off because I don't want to talk about it. "I'll take you home."

She looks around her room sadly. "I don't want—"

I cut off her protest. "It's not safe for you to stay here right now. You'll be safer at home."

"Okay. Thank you."

It's just a ride. Doesn't mean a thing.

SIXTEEN

ATHENA

Athena

Romeo rescued me.

I'm so grateful.

I also feel terrible.

"Romeo, I need to—"

"Don't wanna talk about it, Athena."

"I know. Please let me explain—"

His head snaps up and he glares at me so fierce, my heart thumps. "So were you fuckin' Snake or one of his buddies?" he snarls at me.

"What?" How can he ask me that?

He drops down onto my bed and stares at me. "Well, since you used me to pop your cherry and all, figured you'd be makin' up for lost time."

I have to take a second and process that so I don't smack him. "First, can we stop with the whole *popping cherry* thing, it's so gross."

A slight smile quirks at the corner of his mouth.

I grab more clothes and cram them into my backpack, along with my wallet and a few other small things I don't want to leave behind. I have a feeling I won't be coming back here. Ever. "And no, I didn't. I'm not…I'm not like that. You're my only—" How dare he, when he's got girls crawling all over his clubhouse waiting to jump into his bed. "How many of your club girls serviced you since I left?"

For some reason, that wipes the smirk off his face. "None. And I don't give a fuck if you believe me."

I want to call bullshit. Except, his face is so tight with emotion he doesn't want me to see, it makes me think he might be telling the truth. I stop and sit next to him on the bed, sliding my hand over his. He doesn't snatch his hand back, but he doesn't look at me either.

"You don't like being vulnerable, do you?"

He finally turns his head just enough for me to see the conflict flickering in his dark eyes. "I can't afford to be vulnerable in this life." He slips his hand out from underneath mine and runs the back of his hand over my cheek. "You make me vulnerable."

Oh my God. Did he really just admit that to me? Maybe he doesn't hate me after all. "That's not a bad thing."

"Yeah, it is. Setting aside the whole sneaking out of bed and leaving in the middle of the night with nothing more than a fucking *note* thing—"

"I'm sorry—"

He places his finger over my lips and continues. "Some guy called and told me he was gonna hurt you, and I didn't even hesitate to ride out here with five of my brothers to rescue you. Didn't think about any consequences."

I fidget with my now empty hands in my lap. "Thank you." My voice barely registers over the thundering in my ears. "I'm sorry."

"For what? Sneaking out in the middle of the night? Dragging my club into a war we can't afford?"

"All of it. I didn't think—"

"Yeah, you didn't think. You took your walk on the wild side, got the biker thug to *pop your cherry* and took off."

Wait. He's more than angry. "I hurt your feelings?"

He glares at me. "No."

"Reed, you can be vulnerable with me."

"No. I can't." His gaze roams over my face and I don't think he likes what he sees. "I don't trust you."

"Reed—"

"I asked about your plans. You should have—"

"I thought you'd try to stop me."

"Looks like someone *should* have tried to stop you." The insinuation that I got myself into this mess because I'm so naive—even though it's true—sends fire through my veins. The pissed-off kind of fire that makes me say stupid things.

"You know what? Screw you. I was doing fine out here. If I hadn't met you, this never would have happened."

Whoops. As soon as the words are out of my mouth, I want to yank them back, but it's too late.

He stands, jaw tight, hands fisted. "You're puttin' this on me?" Disbelief drips from every word he spits out.

Stupid pride won't allow me to keep my mouth shut. I stand and face him, fury making me say things I hate, even as they're tumbling off my tongue. "Yes. He saw me wearing *your* shirt, and that's why he got the idea to call *you* for ransom."

"You have any idea what a guy like him would do to you if I'd said no? If I hadn't risked my ass, my club, and a wad of cash to rescue you?"

"I would have told him to call my parents." My voice isn't sure or convincing.

He nods in understanding and smirks. But it's devoid of any humor. "You're one ungrateful little bitch, Athena, you know that?"

"Fuck you. Don't call me a bitch."

He closes in on me, vibrating with such tension, I take a step back. "You're acting like one. You stole my motherfuckin' shirt and somehow that makes it my fault you got yourself in trouble?"

It doesn't make any sense, but I'm too tired and pissed off to check myself. "Yes."

He shakes his head and storms toward the door. "Unbelievable." He turns and gives me one last look. "Get your ass downstairs in the next five minutes or I'm leaving without you."

Suddenly I'm wondering if it's such a good idea for me to go with him.

Five minutes later, I find myself downstairs. He wasn't kidding. He and the guys who came with him are on their bikes, ready to go. Shame washes over me when I wonder how much of our fight they overheard.

I recognize Dante in the group, but I'm too embarrassed to say anything to him. I'm grateful that he thought I was worth saving too. All of these men came here to rescue me because of their loyalty to Romeo, and all I did was say a lot of mean shit to him.

"Reed, I'm sorry. I shouldn't—"

"Get on." He shoves a helmet in my hands and waits until I strap it on myself.

"Wait. What about my car?"

"Prospect will drive it back."

I glance at his bike again. Such a long drive.

"Romeo—"

"Athena, my patience is nil right about now. I need to get you the fuck out of here before the fuckers looking for Snake show up. The less his club knows about you, the safer you'll be."

Reluctantly, I climb on behind him and we take off.

Hours later, I can't take any more. It's hot. I'm starving, sweating, and thirsty. I hurt everywhere from being tied to the bed half the night.

"Romeo. Please, can we stop?" I shout over his shoulder.

Without answering, he pulls off the road. His brothers who'd been traveling with us follow.

"What?" he snaps once he shuts the bike down. I swing my leg over and hop off so fast I almost fall on my ass.

"I can't. I can't do anymore on the bike. I hurt everywhere." I show him my raw wrists, hoping he'll have some mercy on me.

He stares at me for a few seconds before seeming to come to a decision.

"Yeah. Okay."

He stalks over to the other guys and they talk, while I stand there drowning in misery. My head snaps up when the bikes roar to life. Romeo returns by himself and he's definitely not in a talkative mood, so I keep quiet while he studies his phone.

Finally, he glances up. "You need to use the bathroom or something?"

"I guess."

His exasperation with me is clear by the way he waves his hand at the building behind me. I scurry in, do my thing and hurry back before he has a conniption.

I groan when I climb back on the bike, but at least this time we're not riding for long. He pulls into a reasonably decent looking motel, parking by the office. I hop off before he has to ask and follow him inside.

"Two beds," he corrects the desk clerk when he tries to stick us with one king bed.

Great.

Romeo grabs two takeout menus and walks out without even looking at me. This silent treatment is getting annoying.

We stop at his bike and he throws my bag at me without a word, grabs his own stuff, then enters a room near the office.

Inside the doorway, he stops and points at the far bed. "I'll take the bed by the door. You take that one."

"Okay."

I set my bag down and dig through for my toothbrush and something to sleep in.

"Go clean up. I'll order a pizza—if that's okay with you." The way he says it doesn't sound as if it's up for discussion. Without answering, I head into the bathroom.

Once I'm under the hot shower spray, all the events of the past few days slam into me with the force of a brick wall. Refusing to cry in front of Romeo, I've held back all afternoon. The hot water stings my raw wrists, but that's not the reason I slide down to the floor and finally let all my tears free.

Romeo

Athena walks out of the bathroom in a T-shirt I recognize as mine—the one she said started this whole mess, I assume.

Christ, she's got her hair in two braids, punching me in the gut with memories of our time together. Fun, playful, fucking.

Nothing about this situation is fun. And we're definitely *not* fucking tonight. No matter how fucking cute she is in those braids.

Only choice I got is to keep things cool between us. Learned a valuable lesson earlier. While all along I'd been worried I was too old for her, it turned out *she's* too young for *me.*

No fucking way am I going there again. My life was fine before she came into it, and it will be fine again once I get her out of it.

I'm not a complete asshole, though. While she was in

the shower, I ordered pizza, sodas, and ran over to the office for a first aid kit.

I lay out gauze, ointment, and a few other things, while she sits on the end of the bed and finishes braiding her hair.

Her big eyes follow my every movement, so I pretend I don't know she's there. Don't know she's watching. When I'm finished, I flick my hand at her. "Come here."

She scurries over. Eyes still big, and scared. I grab her right hand and check her wrist. Should have taken a better look at it back in California. The skin's red, and bruised, but any bleeding stopped a while ago. Still looks awful and I'm pissed with myself for not getting in a few punches to Snake's face before we left.

I smooth on some ointment and wind a clean piece of gauze around her wrist, secure it, then do the same for her other arm.

The television's loud, drowning out any chance of conversation. When I'm finished bandaging her wrists, she sighs and sits in the chair next to me to eat.

When we're finished, I clean off the table. When I've done every last thing I can to ignore her, I finally spare her a glance. "Get some sleep. We're leaving early in the morning."

"Okay."

She tucks herself into the bed and I barely resist the urge to pull her into my arms, kiss her, and make everything right.

Fuck that.

I kick the bathroom door closed and take one long

motherfuckin' shower, praying like fuck she's asleep when I'm done.

Wish granted.

She's facing away from the light, so I can't take one more look at her pretty face.

I set an alarm, shut everything off, and slide into my bed *alone*.

SEVENTEEN

ATHENA

My chattering teeth wake me. Sleeping in a paper bag would be warmer than under the scratchy motel blanket. I blink a few times and can just barely make out the room. Romeo's in the bed next to me, sound asleep. If I slip in next to him, maybe I can get warm and if I'm lucky, defrost him too.

I pull the covers back and he startles. The bed dips under me, even though I try to move as quietly as possible.

"What're you doing?" he mumbles.

"I'm freezing."

He grunts and turns over, but at least he doesn't kick me out.

Still freezing, I snuggle up against his back, soaking in his warmth.

Somehow I sink back into sleep only to wake sometime later cuddled in Romeo's arms. I almost weep with happiness, until I realize he's still asleep.

Well, at least his subconscious doesn't hate me.

His head's sort of resting on my shoulder, his nose buried against my neck. Warm breath drifts over my skin, comforting me. One of his arms bands around my middle, holding me tight.

I'm almost asleep again when his thumb brushes against my breast. A sharp intake of breath and he seems to come fully awake.

"Athena?"

"Please don't make me leave. I'm cold."

He doesn't answer with words, but his hand slides down my belly, pushing up under my shirt. I let out a hiss of air when his rough hand brushes against my bare stomach, glides over my ribs, and roughly palms my breast.

"Take your shirt off," he demands in a low voice against my ear.

I wriggle out of it and toss it on my bed. While I'm distracted, he takes one nipple between his lips and sucks hard.

"Oh," I gasp in surprise. Then gasp again when his hand dips under my panties, and without any delay, shoves one finger inside me. The sound of how wet I am from being next to him makes me blush. Thankfully he can't see my red cheeks in the dark.

He pulls his hand away and sits up. His fingers dig into my sides as he grabs my underwear, yanking it down my legs.

"Reed?"

He still doesn't say anything. But he shoves his boxer briefs down. The air around us is thick with our heavy breathing. Sex won't save us. It can't. I broke us when I left. And again when he rescued me by running my big mouth. Instead, maybe this can be something new or something to carry with me when we go our separate ways tomorrow.

The thought tightens my throat.

Romeo palms my other breast, rolling my nipple almost to the point of pain. Before I left for California, each time we had sex it was dirty for sure, but it was also fun.

This isn't fun. But at least it's better than the cold indifference he's been giving me all afternoon.

His cock presses against me. Hot and hard. I open my legs wider, lift my hips. Tingles dance up my spine. I want him so much. I want him to make me feel better. I want him to know how sorry I am, even if I can't speak the words.

He thrusts into me with force, and I gasp. The sensations wobble between pain and pleasure, finally landing on *so fucking good.* A soft moan frees itself from my throat as he keeps fucking me. This doesn't remotely resemble making love. It's not even sex. It's angry *fucking.* Every jerk of his hips is about what *he* wants. Not me. He's not even attempting to make it enjoyable for me, but I don't care.

Wet noises fill the tiny room, and I arch my back, trying to gain more friction. His hands clamp over my hips holding me down, not letting me find any relief.

"Reed. Reed, please?"

"Don't," he growls.

I realize why he feels so hot and amazing. "Reed, condom?"

"Fuck." He stops his furious thrusting but doesn't open his eyes.

My fingers trace along his jaw. "It's okay. I...I saw a doctor. Started the pill—" It's so embarrassing to have this conversation with him already inside me. When I'm so confused about where we stand.

His eyes snap open and instead of relief, I see more fury. "That so?"

"I—"

"Well, you got no idea where I've been."

"Don't. Please." I know he's mad, but I don't for a second think he'd deliberately hurt me.

I lift my legs, wrapping them around his waist, and he starts rocking into me again.

I'm so close. "Reed. I'm—"

Abruptly, he pulls out. Searing heat splashes over my thighs and belly. He groans through his release, leaving me stunned, sticky, and unsatisfied.

His labored breathing fills the space of the room. "Reed? I didn't—"

"Sucks for you." He staggers out of bed and into the bathroom, slamming the door behind him.

He returns a few seconds later, fully dressed, and tosses a washcloth at me. "Clean yourself up and get in your own fucking bed."

Too stunned to do anything else, I wipe myself off, and scramble out of his bed. Feeling vulnerable, small, and pathetic, I slip his shirt back on and get under my covers.

"I'm going out. Stay fucking put or I swear to fuck I'll leave without you, and you can find your own fucking way home."

His cold voice and the way he can't even look at me triggers tears to roll down my cheeks. "Reed—"

He finally turns his gaze on me. "Don't fucking call me that again."

Then he's out the door.

And I cry myself to sleep.

Romeo

I've done plenty of fucked-up shit in my life. That scene with Athena has to be one of the worst. I'm so furious I have to get away from her. Even if I don't go farther than the liquor store next door.

A few tiny bottles of Jack Daniels ain't gonna make a dent in my horrible mood. Can't get too drunk anyway. Need to be up early and on the road, not nursing a hangover.

I sprawl out on the plastic chair in front of our room. I need to be away from her, but I can't leave her unprotected either. I'm an asshole for sure, but not that far gone.

Why? Why didn't I kick her out of my bed the second she crawled in it? Why couldn't I let go of my anger for five seconds and treat her better? I hate acting like a pissy man-child because my girl *hurt my feelings*.

My girl.

Fuck. That.

The mild buzz I got going isn't near enough to deal with what's on the other side of the door. But I get up and drag my sorry ass in anyway.

She's curled over on her side. Back to me. My eyes

never leave her as I shut the door. The soft click is louder than I intended, but I don't think she was sleeping. She's too still. Like she's holding her breath.

As I get closer, her shoulder trembles.

She's crying. And what's becoming a familiar feeling of dread fills me. I fucking hate seeing her cry. Worst is knowing I'm responsible for her tears.

Toeing off my boots, I lift up the covers. "Move over."

She slides over without answering. But her breathing hitches and she hiccups out a little sob. Gathering her in my arms, I pull her to my chest. I'd love to feel her bare skin on mine, but I can't take it again. I kiss her cheek instead, her tears salty on my lips.

"I'm sorry," I whisper between kisses.

She shakes and sobs harder. "I'm sorry too. I'm so sorry."

"I know you are."

"I—"

"Shh."

She reaches down and traces her fingers over my arm. I can't tolerate her touch. I use one hand to trap her hands between her breasts and keep my other one on her hip.

"Go to sleep."

"I can't," she cries miserably. The suffering in her voice rips me apart inside.

"You still need to come, baby?"

"Yes," she says as if it kills her to admit it.

I shouldn't. But I can't stop touching her. I can't pull my face away from her hair, from her neck. I'm trying to burn her scent into my nose, because this is *the last time*.

"Lean back."

My hand slides down over her bare stomach, thighs, she never bothered to put her underwear back on after I tossed her out of my bed. "Open."

"No," she whispers, clenching her legs even tighter.

Turns out my big hand wedges in between her legs fine. I pry her open enough to slide my middle finger through her slit.

A soft moan escapes her and she shifts, letting me in.

It doesn't take long until she comes, gasping and shuddering.

"Go to sleep now, baby. Long day tomorrow."

She lets out a sweet sigh and goes soft in my arms. "Thank you."

My lips find her cheek again and at least there are no more tears.

EIGHTEEN

ATHENA

I ROLL over the next morning expecting to collide with a warm, wall of muscle and almost fall out of the bed.

I'm alone.

Did I dream it?

Blinking my eyes open, I take in the motel room.

If it wasn't for my missing underwear and grungy crying hangover, I'd believe last night was just a dream.

Or a nightmare.

First Romeo being so mean. Angry fucking. Him leaving. Him returning, so sweet and tender.

And now I'm waking up alone.

There's a fresh bottle of water on the night stand. I uncap it and take slow sips, replaying last night's events.

"Romeo?" I call out, my voice cracking. Did he make good on his threat and leave me?

Fuck it. I grab my bag and head to the bathroom to dress. I think we've got another three hours on the road, then I can get away from him and think.

I haven't even considered what the hell I'll say to my

parents. I know they're livid with me for leaving. They left me a lot of unhappy voicemails the first week I was in L.A. Like a coward, I kept them updated with daily emails about how I was doing instead of calling them back.

Coward. Well, at least I admit it.

The sound of the motel door slamming shut, hurries me out of the bathroom. Romeo barely glances my way, but points to the table, where he's laid out coffee and maybe a bagel.

"Eat."

I don't know what to say, so for once in my life, I keep my damn mouth shut.

He hardly gives me enough time to choke down the bagel and take a few sips of coffee.

"Let's go. I don't want to make any stops unless we have to."

"Not even the bathroom?" I tease.

Nothing.

I take another chance. "Can we talk first?"

"No."

He turns and leaves. I rush to use the bathroom, one last time apparently, grab my stuff and meet him outside.

With the morning sun shining down on us, this time the ride isn't as awful. I actually enjoy the wind whipping my pony tail behind me and the feel of Reed underneath my fingers.

All too soon, he's turning onto my parents' street. What the hell?

"Romeo, what are you doing?" I shout, when he doesn't bother to shut the bike down in my parents' driveway.

"Bringing you home like I promised."

Why did I assume he'd take me home with him? "But—"

My car's already sitting in the driveway. I can only imagine what my parents must think. What would the prospects who dropped it off have told them? Probably nothing.

"Get off, Athena."

Slowly, I swing my leg up and over the bike, balancing myself on his shoulder.

"We're not going to talk at all?"

"There's nothing to talk about."

"Not even after last night?"

His jaw clenches tight before he answers. "That was a mistake."

He gives me about two seconds to unstrap my bag before taking off, leaving me stranded at my parents' house.

All I can do is watch him drive away.

NINETEEN

ROMEO

"You motherfuckin' prick."

That's rude.

What the fuck?

My head's pounding. Went straight to the clubhouse, ignored every bitch in sight, and proceeded to get stinking drunk.

Something slams into the bottom of whatever I'm sleeping on, jarring me painfully awake.

Dante's angry face stares down at me.

"What the fuck, bro?" My words come out thick and slurred.

"You just dumped Athena at her house without making sure she was okay?"

"She ain't my problem." I roll over without vomiting and consider it a win.

"Like fuck she's not." He kicks the couch again.

"Knock it off, fucker."

"Her parents kicked her out and took her car."

I refuse to let him know how much that bothers me.

"So?" I mumble into the couch cushions. They smell like ass, which makes me reconsider shoving my face against them.

"So, now I got her living at my fuckin' house."

With two hands on my head, to keep it from exploding, I sit up and face him. "Why is this my problem?"

"Are you fuckin' serious? You rode out of here like a fuckin' lunatic. Risked getting' in the middle of Red Storm bullshit to rescue her, and now you're gonna act like you don't give a shit?"

"That about sums it up."

He jams a finger in my chest, knocking me against the back of the couch and I slap it away. "I fuckin' warned you to be careful with her."

"She left. Got her ass in trouble. Obviously, she ain't ol' lady material. So mind your own business."

Dante ignores everything I said. "That's no excuse to be so fuckin' harsh on her. She's eighteen, ya fuck. She knows dick about this life. You knew that going in. Eighteen-year-old girls do stupid shit. Your own fuckin' fault."

"Karina doesn't."

Wrong thing to say. His face goes positively ice-cold. I'd laugh if my head didn't hurt so fucking bad.

"She's different. Leave her out of this."

"What do you want?"

"I want you to treat her with some fuckin' respect and at least talk to her."

I groan and put my head down, although if I vomit on Dante, maybe he'll go away and leave me alone. "Why?"

"Because now I'm outnumbered in my own fuckin' house and I gotta listen to a broken-hearted girl cryin' her eyes out all god damned night long."

What a load of bullshit. I stand, swaying on my feet just a tad, and poke Dante in the chest until he takes a step back. "She ain't broken-hearted. She was doing just fine in California and she'll do just fine here."

"You're a dick."

"So I hear."

"You ain't gonna talk to her?"

"Nope."

He glares at me and when I don't say anything he nods. "Fine. Then you stay the fuck away from her permanently."

"No problem."

"I ain't fuckin' joking. You don't get to decide in a few weeks, when you're done sulking like a pussy, that you wanna start something up again. You won't man up and talk to her now, then you ain't doin' it later."

I open my mouth to say fine again, but nothing comes out.

Dante smirks and folds his arms over his chest.

Motherfucker.

Athena

"I'm so sorry, Karina."

My best friend smiles and sets a plate of cookies in front of me.

"It's okay."

"How mad is Dante that I'm here?"

This time she grins. "He's not mad at all. Flustered maybe."

"I'll find a job and apartment, I promise."

"Are you going back to L.A.?"

I've thought about this endlessly. Romeo doesn't want me. That bridge has been incinerated. I talked to Elliot for over an hour last night. He cheered me up by mentioning, one of the casting directors I'd auditioned for told him she might have a part coming up that was perfect for me. When I pointed out I had no way to get back to Los Angles and nowhere to stay even if I did, he offered money for a bus ticket and invited me to come stay with him. Unsure of what I'd done to deserve his kindness, I'd blubbered out a thank you and promised him I'd think about it.

"Maybe. Elliot's roommate is leaving when their lease is up, so he asked if I want to get an apartment together."

"At least you know he's safe and won't have psychos visiting."

My exact same thoughts when he'd brought it up. "True."

"A gay bestie in Hollywood. You're such a cliché."

My lips twitch into a brief smile. "You're a cliché for saying that."

Her laughter lifts some of the gloom off my shoulders.

My whole body tenses when I hear Dante's bike in the front yard. I'm still mortified Karina had to pick me up from my parents. She brought me here, and forced me to explain the whole story to Dante. Recounting how Romeo dumped me in my parents' driveway like a sack of garbage and how my parents refused to allow me in the house, left me wishing I'd hitchhiked back to Los Angeles instead of calling Karina. What was the point of coming home to a place where no one wanted me?

Well, Karina seems happy I'm here. Staying with the two of them is fucking weird, though. Inside these walls, Dante's completely different. Still bossy and demanding, for sure. But he also dotes on my friend in a way that's sweet and unexpected.

Let's not forget he didn't hesitate to offer me the spare bedroom when Karina dragged me home like a homeless kitten either.

Karina lights up and rushes to the door to greet him. Even though he's only been gone for about an hour, they make out as if he'd been off to war and back. *This* is the weirdness. The two of them can't keep their hands off each other. And I don't even want to contemplate the noises that came from their bedroom last night.

Who wants to nurse a shattered heart around two kinky nymphos?

Not me.

My heavy, dramatic sigh finally pulls them apart. Dante pins me with a stern stare. "You okay?"

"Yeah, it's just getting so hot in here we might need to put the A/C on."

Karina blushes and pulls away from him, while Dante glances up at the ceiling, probably praying for aliens to come abduct me.

Karina pulls him over to the kitchen counter and hands him a cookie, which he devours in two bites. He compliments little Miss Nestle Tollhouse and presses a kiss to her forehead.

Barf.

"How you feelin' today, Athena?" he asks.

"Better. Thank you for—"

He waves off my gratitude. "You can stay here as long as you need to."

"Okay."

"On one condition."

Oh dear God, please tell me this isn't the part where they ask me to join them upstairs.

"You need to stay away from Romeo," he finishes.

I almost would have preferred a three-way invite to hearing Romeo's name. "Uh...no problem there."

"I ain't kidding."

"Okay. Jeez. I think I might go back to L.A. anyway."

Dante's scowl spurs me to explain. "I talked to my friend there and he said I can stay with him. I'll be safe there."

"We'll see." I don't think I care for the ominous tone he uses, but I keep my mouth shut.

Karina bounces on her toes, dying to share her news with Dante. "I heard from Kadence."

He lifts an eyebrow. "And?"

"She wants to meet up tomorrow. Athena said she'll go with me."

Dante's face turns hard and unreadable. "Where?"

"Mall maybe?"

"No. Do it at the clubhouse where I can keep an eye on you. Just in case."

"Are you sure? We could meet here? I can make dinner—"

"Definitely not here." His face softens when he sees the

pout on her face. Why couldn't Romeo be patient and understanding the way Dante is? "I know she's your sister, baby girl. But you don't know a thing about her. I don't trust her enough to have her in my home."

The man has a point, and I'm about to say that when Karina agrees.

Oh fuck. That means— "Karina, you don't still need me then, do you?"

"Yeah," Dante answers. "You should still be there for her."

Karina nods vigorously. How can I say no?

"But you just said you wanted me to stay away from Romeo," I point out.

Dante's not used to having people—girls specifically, I think—question him. "I'll make sure he doesn't bother you," he answers slowly, giving me a hard look. "I'd like you there for Karina's sake."

Shit. Guilt me much? "Yeah, no problem."

As long as I avoid Romeo, everything will be fine.

TWENTY

ROMEO

It's a shame I have to kill Dante.

We've been brothers for almost twenty years. Sure, we annoy the fuck out of each other, but our friendship goes back before patching into the club. Bonded over all the dirty deeds we were forced to do as prospects. Patched in at the same time. Even got elected to our current positions at the same time.

What he's doing today can't go unpunished though.

"Why are they in my clubhouse?" I growl at him.

He's probably smirking at me. But I can't tell because my eyes haven't left Athena since she walked in here with Dante's girl a couple minutes ago.

"Karina's meetin' up with her sister."

"That still doesn't answer my question."

"I want Athena here for moral support, in case things don't go well."

"That doesn't explain why they're in *my clubhouse*."

"Well, Prez," he answers slowly. "I don't want Kadence up at *my* house yet."

I'd love to punch the sarcasm out of him. "But having her in our clubhouse seems safe? You know she's got ties to Bolt's crew."

"Ain't like they don't know where our clubhouse is, Prez."

He's got a point.

Still, I want Athena out of my clubhouse.

Or upstairs in my bed.

I tell myself it's her outfit that's messing with my head. Some sort of skintight pants with little cupcakes printed all over them and a loose pink tank top.

I want to eat every inch of her.

Kadence finally shows up, and Dante leaves to supervise his girl. The sisters have a tearful first meeting. At least they finally know about each other. Tucker made a big deal about how wild Kadence is, and by the look of her, he wasn't just saying it to be an asshole. She screams trouble. From her barely-there top to the shorts that barely cover her ass cheeks. That's how she goes dressed to an MC clubhouse during the day to meet her sister? A rival of her man's MC too, from what I hear. I don't envy Dante for having to deal with *that* bullshit.

He must deem Kadence worthy to associate with Karina and finally stops hovering over them. Unfortunately, he returns to annoy me.

"Remember what I said, Prez?"

"Why are you still bothering me?"

The fucker laughs and slaps me on the back.

"Get your drooling in now. I hear she's going back to L.A."

That finally snaps me out of leering at Athena's ass. "What?"

"Yeah. Got some dude lined up to be her roommate and everything."

"Like fuck."

"Not your problem. Remember?"

"Fuck off." I glance at him. "Why're you lettin' her go back there?"

"She wants to go. How am I supposed to stop her?" He lifts his chin in Karina's direction. "I got my hands full with my own girl. Anyway, Athena's not your problem, so don't worry about it."

I wait until Dante's distracted and Athena steps away to make my move. Creepy fuck that I am, I stalk her across the clubhouse. My last threads of patience fray as I wait outside the bathroom. What the fuck do I say? Why am I doing this? We're totally wrong for each other.

She's eight-fucking-teen. Legal, to fuck, sure.

But for fuck's sake, she was a toddler when I patched into the club.

That alone should be enough to keep me away from her.

Except, my moral compass has been off-kilter for as long as I remember.

I should leave her alone and let her find a man who makes more sense for her.

The thought of her with anyone else pushes me into jealous asshole territory.

When the door finally opens, I'm wound so tight, I grab her and throw her up against the wall. She lets out a startled gasp of surprise.

"Why're you in my clubhouse?" I ask, my lips so close to hers, I can almost taste her.

"I—I'm with Karina," she stammers, those gorgeous steel blues wide as saucers. "Dante said it was okay and you wouldn't bother me."

"Am I *bothering* you, sweetheart?"

Her eyes gloss over. "No. But you're hurting me."

I relax my hold on her but still keep her trapped against the wall with my body. "Sorry."

"What do you want from me?" she asks with a hitch in her voice.

"I don't know."

"Well, if you don't know, how should I?" She tries to push her way out from under me, but I keep her pinned. Missed that smart mouth.

"I want to stop thinking about you all the fucking time," I admit.

Her eyebrows scrunch into an adorable little crinkle. "Yeah? Well, me too."

"You think about you all the time, too?"

"Don't be a jerk."

"I'm still pissed you left the way you did."

She looks down at where our bodies are almost touching. "I know. I'm still mad at myself."

I'm surprised to hear her admit that.

"Why'd you do it?"

"I don't know. I can't explain it. It'd been my dream for so long, I was afraid if I gave it up for a guy and then it didn't work out, I'd be a failure."

Her honesty breaks some of my anger. "I wish you'd talked to me about it."

"I didn't think you were serious about me staying."

"Yeah, I get that."

"I tried calling—"

"I know."

"I—"

I cut her off with a kiss. At first she kisses me back, but then she shakes herself free. "Don't do this to me again. Please," she whispers.

"Do what?"

She lowers her gaze. "Confuse me."

I know she's referring to our night in the motel and guilt slams into me. "You're the one in *my* clubhouse," I say instead of what I should say.

"I didn't mean—"

"No? What'd you mean? Coming here dressed like that."

"Like what?"

"So fucking sexy I can't take my eyes off you."

"Let go of me and I'll get out of your sight."

My arms tighten around her. "No." I cup her face in my hands and crush my mouth to hers. Our kisses meld into one long hungry kiss until we're both breathing hard. She shudders as one of my hands kneads her breast and whimpers as my fingers trail down her side, slipping under the whispy fabric of her shirt. For a second, I work my fingers over her skin, I missed her softness.

"Put your hands on my shoulders."

She stares at me with dazed eyes. "Why?"

"I want to find out how wet you are."

I don't wait for an answer. I tug at the stretchy waistband of her pants and slip my hand inside.

She gasps as I force my hand between her thighs, touching everywhere. "Is this mine?"

"God, yes."

Athena

I can't think straight. I might even pass out.

Is this really happening?

I almost died when I walked into the clubhouse and saw Romeo. The heavy weight of his gaze sat on my shoulders the entire time Karina and Kadence were talking, until the need to get away and take some deep breaths chased me out of the room.

Then he grabbed me, admitted he can't stop thinking about me either. Kissed me.

And now his hand's down my pants cupping my pussy in a thrilling possessive way that makes my heart race.

"Is this mine?" He growls the question against my throat again and I think I gasp out an answer, but I'm not sure.

"Answer me and I'll make you come." Despite the possessive grip on my private parts, he rains soft kisses on my cheeks, forehead, and finally my lips. "Would you like that?" he asks.

My lips part as I stare at his wicked smirk. "Only yours."

"I can't stand thinking of you with anyone else," he admits.

"Me either."

"There's no one but you, Shortcake."

Oh. The rough way he whispers the silly, but sweet

nickname makes my nipples tighten. Then the rest of his sentence registers. "No. I mean, I can't stand the idea of being with anyone besides you. Ever."

He studies me for second. I meant every word though. I know he thinks I'm too young to know what the hell I want. But if I try to picture myself in five, ten, or twenty years, I can't see anything that doesn't include his arms around me. It's the only place I've ever felt completely safe. Even when he's tense and so on the edge his grip is less than gentle. I don't need gentle. I need strong, determined, and protective.

"Careful, Athena," he warns. "I want to do what's right for you, but when you say stuff like that, it's hard."

I'm not sure what he thinks is *right* for me, but then his hand presses into me, the tips of his fingers sliding up my slit and nothing else matters. He buries his face against my neck, kissing and licking.

"Romeo. Someone…someone might see us."

"So." He slides his fingers right up to my clit and I gasp, jerking my hips into his hands. "You're soaked," he whispers. "I think the idea of someone seeing me doing dirty things to you turns you on."

He traces a lazy circle around my clit before working his way back. Up and down he teases me. Slipping his fingers inside me, then taking them away.

My skin flames. Scared we might get caught. Secretly thrilled at the idea. The teasing stops and he slides one finger inside me, so hard I let out a soft squeak. Every confident stroke pushes me closer to the edge.

"Tell me what you need, Athena. Say it."

"This. Please don't stop."

"Harder?" He adds another finger, giving me an extra little push that makes me rise on tip toes.

"Yes, yes. So good. Like that."

"I need you in my bed, Athena. Need to fuck you. Need you to know you're mine."

Those words give me the extra nudge I need. My skin burns all over, and I shudder through my orgasm. He kisses my forehead and holds me until I stop trembling.

"Beautiful."

Romeo

If I don't get her upstairs soon, we'll end up rutting in the hallway like animals.

"I got you, Shortcake. Ride it out."

She responds by melting into me, wrapping her arms around my neck. I lift her into my arms and carry her upstairs.

By the time I get her to my room, she's coherent again. She claws at my shirt as I set her down and I whip off her top. She rubs her hand over my dick, still trapped in my pants.

"I want to take care of you."

"Not yet, Shortcake. This is still all about you." I take a step back to admire the sight of her innocent pink bra and those *fucking cupcake pants*.

"These fucking pants have been messing with me since you got here," I say as I sink to the floor in front of her and peel the soft, stretchy material down her legs.

"You like them?" she asks, her sex-kitten tone making a reappearance.

"Yup." I trace my fingers under the tiny pink thong she's wearing. "This is nice, too."

She giggles, then gasps as I slide them down her legs, and put my mouth on her.

"Get on the bed," I mumble against her pussy after giving it one final lick. She races over and jumps into my bed. Her big blue eyes watch intently as I set a record for shedding my clothes.

I want to shove my face in her cunt and lick her until she screams, but I start slow, kissing my way down her body. Savoring every inch. Everything about her is beautiful and I feel like a brute attacking her.

"Missed you," I mumble against her breast.

Her hands rake through my hair, sending shivers down my spine. "I missed you too, Reed. So much."

There hasn't been a whole lot of forgiveness in my world, but for her I'll make an exception.

Athena

After blowing my mind, Reed kisses his way up my body. My head lolls to the side, and I spot the camera.

"Did you film someone else?"

"What?" he asks completely confused.

I point to the camera.

"No. Fuck no, you fucking brat. Since the real thing was gone, all I had was that motherfucking video to watch and jack off to."

Okay, even with all crudeness, there's something sweet in that sentence. "You really didn't have anyone else up here?"

"No, I really didn't," he answers as if he's both pissed and surprised with himself. He presses his forehead to mine and closes his eyes. "I'm in love with you, Athena. So, no. There was no one else."

For a second, there's no air in my lungs. No sound touches my ears. Nothing but the heat and weight of him above me.

"I don't need you to say it. But I need you to know it."

"I'm scared," I admit.

His expression softens. "Why're you scared, sweetheart?"

"You're—"

"So much fucking older than you?"

"Well, yeah."

He chuckles and lifts one of my legs, bringing my knee up to his hip and pushing inside me until I moan.

"Scares me too. You're gonna realize you don't belong with me."

"I don't want kids," I blurt out.

He shakes with laughter and ducks his head. "Neither do I."

"Right now. I mean, in a few years I might."

He chuckles against my neck as he lazily slides in and out of me.

"I think I want to go back to L.A."

"Yeah, I heard. Planning to live with some guy?" he growls out the words and slams into me a little harder as he says it.

"Who told you that?"

"Never mind. Is it true?"

"He's gay. And he helped me a lot out there."

"We'll see. Now pipe down and fuck me. We'll figure it out later."

I groan as I slide into oblivion. He reaches over and flicks the camera on.

"You mean that?" I ask.

"Fuck yeah." He brushes a kiss over my forehead. "I want you to be happy, Athena."

His hips flex and he slams into me so hard, I move half-way up the bed. "Oh, fuck that's good, Reed," I moan, our conversation completely evaporating from my mind.

Being underneath him sharpens our differences. He's so big and hard. Powerful. Even with him riding me hard, I feel tiny and cherished.

"Are you still mad at me?" I ask.

"Yeah, probably."

"Taking it out on my pussy?"

His eyes bore into mine. "Fuck yeah. I went easy on you before, Shortcake."

"Good." I bring my hands up to the sides of his face. "Don't hold back."

His raw roughness excites me as much, if not more, than anything else we've done. "Harder."

He pulls out and flips me over, lifts my hips and shoves a bunch of pillows under me, then slams back inside. His hand gathers my hair, gripping and pulling until I have no choice but to turn.

"Careful what you ask for."

I smile back at him. "Bring it."

A growl rips out of his throat. Without leaving my body, he turns us so we're facing the camera and tugs on my hair. "Look into the camera. Wanna catch your face when you come with my cock buried in you."

Imagining him watching this later. Thinking about this moment we had together. I want him to have a good show.

So I look right into the camera and smile.

TWENTY-ONE

ROMEO

WE STAY WRAPPED up in each other for a long time.

After a lot of annoying texts from Dante, asking if Athena's okay, I finally answer him.

Athena sighs and rolls over, slipping her arms around me. "Don't tell me you have to go."

I shut the phone off and set it down. Anyone needs me, I guess they'll have to come knocking.

"No."

She picks her head up, messy blonde hair, spilling over her shoulders, tickling my chest. "Oh my God. Karina's going to kill me. Her sister's going to think—"

"What?"

"I'm such a slut."

I side my hand under her and lift her on top of me. "Yeah, *my* little slut."

"Mmm…I like that. I think you still have a lot of dirty things to teach me."

My dick agrees, stirring to life and she rocks against it. "I'll teach you whatever you want to know."

"Is that wrong?" she asks softly.

"Fuck no." I rub my thumb over her cheek. "Nothing between us, nothing we do together, is wrong."

I cup the back of her head, pulling her in for another kiss. "Would you like to come see my shop tomorrow?"

"You still want me to?"

I have to give it some thought. Before she took off on me, I wanted her there. I think we've straightened things out. "Yeah."

Eventually, we make our way downstairs. Dante smirks at our intertwined hands and I wonder how much of his "stay away from her" threat was designed to push us together. Pointless really, I don't need my friend telling me she's off-limits to make me want her.

"Work things out, Prez?" Wolf asks with a smirk.

I don't need to answer. My fuck-off stare works wonders.

Some of the girls decide to throw together a barbeque out back. The prospects get a work out, carrying shit from the kitchen to the patio. Athena leaves my side to join Karina. Dante's stealthy ass sneaks up on me.

"Is she staying?" he asks.

"I don't know. We'll figure out the logistics later."

Dante shakes his head.

"But you can drop her stuff off here if you want her out of your house."

"Yeah. Let's give it a day, Prez."

Bold fucker.

I'm not insulted though. He's looking out for Athena and that's a good thing.

"Kadence still here?" I ask.

Dante rolls his eyes before answering. "Yeah."

"How's that workin' out?"

"We'll see."

Athena

Karina's wearing such a smug smile, I approach her carefully.

"Surprised you can walk," she greets me.

"You're one to talk."

Kadence joins us and eyes me up and down. "The president? Aren't you a go-getter."

I flash a weak smile. I still haven't decided if I like her or not.

"Although," she continues. "Bikers are bullshit." She points at Karina, then me. "You two don't have a fucking clue what you're getting into."

Karina's forehead wrinkles, but she doesn't respond.

Not bothered by her sister's silence, Kadence throws a hostile glance around the open room. "They're bossy, demanding, and have ridiculous double-standards about women."

"Sounds like you're hung up on one particular biker to me," Karina says.

Kadence turns her big sister glare on Karina. "Careful, little sister." Her eyes narrow. "Did he explain how the Iron Bulls claim their ol' ladies yet?" she asks, nodding at Dante.

I watch, fascinated as Karina's cheeks turn a deep pink. "Yes."

"Wait. What do they do?" I ask.

Kadence lifts her chin at the closed chapel doors. "They fuck you on the table in front of everyone."

Whoa. Prickles of heat race over my skin. My eyes seek Romeo out. Casually leaning against the wall, talking to Dante. He nods and one corner of his mouth lifts when our eyes meet. Glancing around the room I take in the other brothers. What would it be like to have Romeo give a very visual explanation of how I only belong to him? Would he bend me over the table in front of everyone? Would the guys sit in their chairs and just watch or would Romeo make them stand on the other side of the room? Would he have me strip naked in front of all his brothers?

The possibilities dance through my head, leaving me a little dizzy.

Karina smacks her sister's arm. "Mind your own business."

"Just looking out for you, little sis."

"I already knew."

"You did?" I ask, my voice about ten decibels louder than necessary. Wow.

Karina blushes an even deeper shade of red. "Dante explained it to me after graduation." She glares at her sister. "He doesn't think I'm ready for it yet, so he wants to wait. But thanks for your concern, sis."

Kadence isn't bothered by the anger coloring Karina's words. The two of them might not have been raised together but they're like the difference between a hurricane and a blizzard. Both destructive weather that cause damage in different ways. Kadence's anger seems to simmer right below the surface, while Karina has much more of a slow burn temper. I know because I've been on the receiving end of it once or twice in our many years of friendship.

I have a million more questions about this claiming thing, but I don't want to ask in front of Kadence.

"Is that how they do it in your ex's club? Is that why you broke up?" Karina asks

Kadence shakes her head and in a minute I know why. Romeo's arm slips around my waist. "You girls all right?"

Despite her obvious dislike of the club, Kadence smiles brightly at Romeo and I'm overcome with an urge to, oh I don't know, scratch her eyes out for being a little too flirty with my man.

"Thanks for letting me hang out in your club, sir," Kadence says while batting her lashes.

Romeo doesn't seem affected by her act. He smirks in response. "Dante didn't give me much choice."

Hah.

Kadence smiles wide and innocent. "We were just talking about the claiming ceremony you guys have here."

"That so?" Romeo glances at me, and I shrug.

"I figured you'd tell me when you were ready."

My response seems to relax him and he ushers us outside for dinner.

After a few drinks, Kadence drops her hostility and we actually have fun. The three of us make plans to go out when Karina's summer classes are over.

After dinner, Romeo pulls me away from the girls, into the shadows where we sort of dance to the music filling the yard. It's sweet and romantic—and surprises me.

"Do you have any questions?"

"About what?"

We stop moving and he glances down at me with a raised eyebrow. My cheeks warm and a smile stretches my mouth. "About you fucking me on the table in front of your club?"

He bursts out laughing. "Yeah, Shortcake. About that."

"Um, only about a hundred."

He nods for me to fire away, so I do. "Do I have to have sex with anyone else?"

"Absolutely not."

"Do other old ladies watch or is it just the brothers?"

"Just the brothers."

Something occurs to me and I slow down my questions. Actually, stop them all together. He hasn't exactly asked me to be his old lady.

"Sorry. I didn't mean to—"

Rough fingers tip my chin up until I'm staring into his eyes. "I'm glad it doesn't bother you."

Okay then.

TWENTY-TWO

ROMEO

THE GUYS ARE ABOUT to take their lunch break when Athena and I arrive at my shop. Perfect.

I stop one of the mechanics, Locke, before he leaves. "Is bay eighteen—,"

"Yup. Waitin' on the special order to finish it up."

"Thanks."

He raises an eyebrow at Athena, so I introduce them. Not that any of the guys need to know a damn thing about my girl.

"You must be special. Boss has never brought a girl here."

Athena beams, while I glare at Locke until he leaves.

"Come here, I wanna show you something."

"I've already seen it."

"What?" Realizing she's messin' with me, I tug her close and smack her ass. She giggles and skips out of my hold.

"Boss, Prez, is there anywhere you're *not* in charge, Reed?"

"No. Now get your ass over here, I want to show you something."

Still laughing, she follows me to the last open garage door. "Oh, wow. It's so pretty."

She walks around the car, careful not to touch it. "It's beautiful."

When she's within reach, I grab her and yank her to me. Then we're mouth-to-mouth. Her arms slide around my neck, and I pick her up and set her on the back of the car. We're still kissing and she skims her hands under my shirt. My body shudders from her touch. I can't get enough of this girl. She pulls away and moves to take her top off, but I stop her.

"No. Don't want any of these fuckers seeing you."

"Oh."

Then we're right back at it. Her fingers twist in my hair as she keeps me close. My hands slide up under her skirt, fingers hooking into her panties and dragging them down her legs. Her hands fumble with my belt and I decide I need her tits in my mouth, so off her shirt goes. Bra too.

"I thought you didn't want anyone to see." She gasps as I lash one hard nipple with my tongue.

"Fuck it. Let them see what they can't have." My fingers brush against a condom in my pocket, and I take a second to roll it on.

She laughs, then gasps, when I spread her knees, lift her up, and thrust into her. I get a little lost staring into her eyes. My movements slow, and she rakes her nails over my scalp. "I love you, Reed."

VEXED

It's the first time she's said it, and I can't imagine a better time or place.

"Love you too, Shortcake." Our lips meet for a long, slow kiss.

When we part, she lies back against the curved glass of the back window, letting me see the way her tits jiggle when I slam into her.

"Like that?" I ask.

"Yes," she answers breathlessly.

"You're so fucking hot. You gonna be mad if someone sees me fucking you?"

"God, no."

The car's low, making it an odd angle for me. I pull out, drag her off the car, bend her over it, lift up her hips, and thrust into her from behind. "Fuck, Reed!"

"Take it for me, Athena."

She's too busy moaning and grinding back against my dick to give me any lip.

"Come for me, sweetheart."

She doesn't answer, but a few seconds later, she moans even louder, clenches so hard around me, I have no choice but to let go. The blissed-out feeling goes on and on as I empty into her.

"Holy fuck."

She gasps and leans against the car. "Oh my God. That was intense."

I lean over and press a quick kiss to her lips. "Yes, it was."

After dropping the condom in one of the trashcans, I find her still slumped against the car. I reach out and run my fingers over her cheek, and help her into her clothes.

She nods at the trashcan. "Thank you."

Knowing exactly what she means, I nod. I wrap my hands around her waist and pull her close. "Figured since I stole your underwear, least I could do is make sure you're not running around with my cum dripping down your legs."

"Damn, you're dirty," she whispers.

I take her mouth in a kiss and give her ass a squeeze.

When we part, she's flushed, and I contemplate taking her into my office. Maybe spreading her out on my desk—

Her voice interrupts my dirty desk fantasy. "I think we left sex prints all over this car. Is the owner going to be mad?"

"I dunno. You tell me." I dig out a key and hand it over.

"What's this? What are you—"

"You need something to get back and forth to L.A."

"It's *mine*? You got me my seventy-six Corvette?" Her voice keeps rising in pitch as the pieces fall into place for her.

"Well, someone brought in as a trade, and I've been fixing—"

She squeals and jumps up to hug me. "Oh my God! That's...thank you."

Fuck, do I love her. "Sparkly paint's coming this week. And Locke's been practicing his Strawberry Shortcakes." Man, has he been pissed about that, too.

Her eyes shine with unshed tears. "I mentioned that *once*. One time, Reed. The night we...got together. And you remembered?"

"Fuck yeah. Silliest thing I ever heard. Fucking cute as hell, though."

She hugs me again. "You really don't mind me going back to L.A.?"

"Yeah, I fuckin' mind. But I'll visit you and you'll come home. Then, when you're a big movie star, you can buy us a house half way." I brush a few loose curls off her cheek. "Nothing else matters as long as you're mine."

"I'm yours. I'm so yours." She reaches up and gives me another kiss. When we part, she glances at the car again. "Thank you, Reed."

"Anything for you, Shortcake."

TWENTY-THREE

ATHENA

Six months later...

"Hurry up, Biker Barbie, Ken's going to be here any minute," Elliot shouts.

"You better not call him that to his face," I warn as I join him in the living room. Romeo's accepted Elliot as my roommate, even if he doesn't always appreciate Elliot's sense of humor.

"Wouldn't dream of it." He runs his skeptical gaze over my cupcake leggings. "What are you wearing? Pajamas? At least pretend you're not going to fuck as soon as you see each other."

"Shut up. He likes these."

The buzzer downstairs goes off and my heart races. Sure enough, a few seconds later, Romeo's knocking at the door. We don't speak at first. I throw myself against him and he catches me, lifting me up, pulling me against him. Our mouths meet and get reacquainted while everything else fades away.

Elliot clears his throat and I draw back.

"I'd leave you two alone, but you're kinda blocking the door."

Romeo's mouth slides into a smirk and he holds his hand out to Elliot for a quick shake. "Good to see you, kid. My girl been behaving?"

"Hey," I protest, smacking Romeo's arm.

Elliot shakes his head. "Not one bit."

"Shut up," I grumble, but I'm laughing too.

Elliot leans over and gives me a brief hug. "Have a safe trip home. See you in a few weeks?"

"Yup."

Romeo watches Elliot leave. Once the door shuts, he pounces, grabbing me and carrying me into the bedroom.

"Missed the fuck out of you," he mumbles against my mouth.

LATER, when we're properly worn out, he leads me downstairs to the garage where my car's stored.

"You want to drive my car home?"

"Yeah. I'll leave this bike in your garage."

I notice it's not his regular ride. This one is devoid of any Iron Bulls MC logos or colors. The respectful way to ride through territories claimed by other clubs, Romeo's explained to me.

The drive home doesn't seem as long when we're together. He drives while I tell him all my stories from the set of the television show I've been working on. It's nothing major. A tiny, tiny recurring role on a big show.

Okay, it's a big deal. The pay is shit, but I'm meeting lots of people.

While the show's on a break from filming, there's nowhere else I'd rather be than with Romeo. Even if it is at the clubhouse.

Except, he goes right past the turn-off for the Iron Bulls compound. "Where are we going?"

"You'll see."

"Are we going to Dante and Karina's?" I have plans with Karina for the day after tomorrow. Tonight and tomorrow are reserved exclusively for my man.

"No."

We pass Dante's driveway, and still Romeo continues into the mountains. Finally, he turns into a long driveway and it's a long way before a house comes into view.

"Where are we?"

"You'll see."

It's a modest log cabin-type of home on the outside. There's nothing modest about the inside though. High-end kitchen, a wall of windows that looks out over the mountains, a spiral staircase to the top floor. It's not completely furnished yet. "It's beautiful, but whose is it?" I ask.

"Mine," Romeo answers. "Ours."

"*Ohmygod!*" While I don't mind being at the clubhouse, sometimes it's a bit much on my short visits home. I've never complained about it. My eyes burn with unshed tears and my lip quivers. He just *knew*.

He takes my hand and leads me downstairs. "What's down here?"

"My favorite part."

He leads me into a room and slides a switch by the door up, illuminating enough for me to see it's a home theater.

"This is so cool."

I'm walking through the space, touching the wide, leather theater-style seats when I notice Romeo slide the doors closed and dim the lights again.

"Have a seat."

"Are we watching something now?"

"Oh, yeah. Been waitin' way too long to watch this with you."

Confused, I take one of the seats in the middle of the room. The chairs are big enough, that Romeo settles in next to me. Our shoulders and thighs press together and I tuck one of my hands under his elbow.

"Ready?" he asks.

And I know what's coming.

Us.

I've watched myself onscreen a few times. The television show.

This is mature content, only appropriate for us. I don't look half bad, shyly posing and teasing him. But when he sets the camera down and comes into view.

Wow.

"Fuck, you're hot," I mutter.

Next to me, Romeo chuckles. His hand moves over my thigh, between my legs.

By the time the film gets to the good stuff, we're not

even looking at the screen. We're way too entwined in each other.

"Think we'll ever watch it to the end?" I ask between kisses.

Against my mouth he smiles. "Probably not."

ALSO BY PHOENYX SLAUGHTER

Asunder (Iron Bulls MC #1)

Disconnect (Iron Bulls MC #2)

Entwined (Iron Bulls MC #3)

Vexed (Iron Bulls MC #4)

Unhinged (Iron Bulls MC #5)

Dirty Side Down (Iron Bulls MC Box Set #1)

Infatuation (A Rebel Stepbrother Romance)